A Deal with a Cruel Earl

HISTORICAL REGENCY ROMANCE NOVEL

Dorothy Sheldon

Table of Contents

Chapter One

The Assembly Rooms Hall, Derby, the Last Ball of the Season

It wouldn't be a ball, of course, without at least a bit of salacious gossip. And the final ball of the magnificent London Season simply *had* to go out with a bang.

A knot of young women had gathered in the corner of the ballroom, the ones not dancing for the current set, and leaned close together. Strawberry blonde curls mingled with thick dark locks, and a head of shining gold stood above it all.

"Have you heard," Cynthia Roland of the strawberry blonde hair said, in a hushed whisper, "about Lady Penelope Black?"

"No, I haven't," responded a golden-haired young woman by the name of Blanche. "Do tell."

"Well, we all know how Penelope has been the darling of the Season. The most beautiful woman in London, they said." Cynthia gave a disdainful sniff. "Fair beauties are the fashion now, but if the gentlemen *will* dote over a black-haired chit like *her*, then..."

"Lady Penelope was very charming," put in a third young woman, a round-faced, dark-haired girl by the name of Miss Prudence Copperwell. "I met her a few times, and she *was* very likeable."

Cynthia scowled at her friend. "I daresay she knew how to *appear* charming. But you all just wait till I tell you what I have to say. She was caught running around in the woods, *alone*, with a gentleman. Shocking, is it not?"

"Oh, goodness," Blanche breathed. "She'll be ruined."

"She is," Cynthia said, with a hint of smugness. "I have it on good authority that she's being sent to her aunt's home in Bath, in deep disgrace. Such a shame – she was doing so well this Season. Although, of course, she hadn't had many offers, so..."

Cynthia trailed off, and there was a moment of awkward silence between the three girls. None of them had received any offers of marriage which had been accepted, and none of any real note. Prudence – affectionately called *Prudy* by her friends and family – privately did not mind. The gentlemen she saw in London were always rather tiresome, and she was quite happy to let her older sister take the spotlight as she wished. Much easier. Besides, who would look at Prudy besides *Catherine*?

"It gets worse," Cynthia continued, recovering herself. "She wouldn't have been caught, you know, if she hadn't come screaming out of the woods, shouting that there was a monster chasing her."

Prudy spluttered, choking on her cup of punch. "A *monster*? Oh, that is ridiculous. How can one be so stupid?"

Cynthia scowled. "This was in Dalton Woods."

"So?"

"So, everybody knows there *is* a monster in that part of the woods. It's very near Rycroft Hall, and there *is* a monster there."

"Are you sure it isn't haunted?" Prudy taunted, lifting an eyebrow.

Her friend narrowed her eyes at her. "Everybody says so. There are dead animals found there, all over, as if they'd fallen from the sky... or dropped dead in shock and fear."

"Perhaps somebody hunts there. A poacher, perhaps." Prudy countered.

"And left their game? I don't think so. I, for one, believe that there *is* a monster there, and that it's hunting for *sport*."

Blanche, always easily frightened, gave a shuddering squeal, pressing her hands to her face.

"Oh, she could have been torn limb from limb!"

"This isn't a monster," Prudy said firmly. "The stupid girl probably saw a shadow, and let her imagination run away with her."

Blanche considered this, nibbling her full lower lip. It was a source of some annoyance between the three girls that Blanche was by far the most beautiful among them. She was, however, also the stupidest, and that had to count for *something*. All told, men did not want silly wives.

Or so Cynthia kept saying, whenever the two of them spent time together without the ever-perfect Blanche.

"But Lady Penelope must be in so much trouble," Blanche said at last. "Her life is ruined, all for one silly mistake. I do feel sorry for her."

"I don't," Cynthia said, snorting. "None of this would have happened if she had just obeyed her parents and followed the

4

rules. Those rules are there for a reason. Ladies' reputations are like glass – easily shattered, and not soon repaired."

She punctuated this point with a nod and a noisy slurp of her tea.

Prudy shifted on her seat. The subject of Lady Penelope's downfall and her imaginary monster – there was no doubt in her mind that it *was* imaginary – was ruining their evening. The Season was ending, and Prudy was determined to wring the last drops of enjoyment out of it, before the winter set in for good.

"Enough of this," she said, setting aside her punch. "I can't believe that neither of you have mentioned my gown. It's the latest fashion in Paris, but I daresay we won't see it until next Season now."

The young ladies required no further persuasion and commenced to exclaim and admire the delicate, mint-hued lace and soft crimson of Prudy's gown. It was brand new and horribly expensive, but her father had never balked at paying for expensive trinkets and fabrics to clothe his two children. Prudy was aware that a beautiful dress could not make her stand beside her sister, but it was something, wasn't it? Besides, Catherine deserved her good looks, because she was pretty inside, too.

Cynthia might turn green with jealousy over Catherine's glossy, chestnut-brown locks, perfect pale skin, impeccable figure and large, green-blue eyes, but Prudy was proud of her sister. Extremely proud.

"Catherine's dress is even prettier!" Blanche exclaimed, straightening up and beaming. The other two glanced up to see a staggeringly beautiful young woman in a sleek, royal blue gown gliding towards them. Her gown was noticeably less frilly and ornamented than Prudy's, and yet she could easily have been considered the prettiest woman in the world.

"Lord, that dance has fatigued me," Catherine sighed, flopping down on a chair beside her sister. "Prudy, can I drink the rest of your punch?"

"Of course! Shall I fetch you some more?"

"Lord Everton seems very taken with you," Cynthia said smoothly. "Isn't that the second dance he's asked for?"

"Only the first," Catherine responded, smiling coolly back. "He asked for a second dance, but I have complained of fatigue.

I'm finished dancing tonight."

Cynthia pouted, sitting back in her seat and crossing her arms.

"We were talking of Lady Penelope Black," Prudy explained. "Isn't it the most deliciously shocking thing? Like something you'd read in a novel."

"The only shocking thing here is the girl's lack of propriety," Cynthia muttered, and Blanche tittered obediently.

Catherine did not smile, picking at the cuffs of her dress.

"You shouldn't gossip about that," she said quietly. "Lady Penelope is ruined. It's hardly something to giggle over, and nothing we should be discussing at all. I pity her, and so should you."

Prudy felt a niggling knot of guilt in her chest, the way she always did when Catherine disapproved of something she said or did. It passed quickly, of course.

"She said something about a monster in Dalton Woods," Prudy continued eagerly, swallowing down her discomfort. "Ridiculous, isn't it?"

"It's said that Rycroft Hall is haunted," Cynthia insisted.

Catherine shook her head. "It's a forbidding place, to be sure. An old building, the sort of place the Gothic castles in those novels you all love to read are modelled on. But there's nothing wrong with the place, it's just a little gloomy."

"So, no monsters?"

"No, Prudy. No monsters."

Prudy shot Cynthia a triumphant glance and received a glare in return. Then Cynthia's gaze slid over her head, and she stiffened.

"Oh. Mr Bates is coming over."

"To speak with Prudy, no doubt," Blanche added, and the two girls shared a quick, malicious glance. It made Prudy feel uncomfortable and left out, for some reason. She glanced at her sister for reassurance, but Catherine was staring into space, a light frown line between her brows, so there was no comfort to be had there.

Then Mr Isaac Bates was upon them.

"Miss Prudence, you are looking lovely tonight," he said breathlessly, smoothing one hand down a shockingly expensive-looking waistcoat.

6

Isaac Bates, at the age of twenty-eight, was an orphan, heir to a shockingly huge fortune, part of an ancient and well-respected family. This, of course, made him a target for every unscrupulous fortune-hunting female in the country. He neatly avoided them all, with surprising grace for such an awkward, stocky young man.

He was of middling height, strongly built, like a farmer instead of a dandy, and wore his fine silks and satins with a hint of discomfort. He was known to be of moderate habits, never in his cups, never passing out in his clubs, and not a flirt. Frankly, Prudy wasn't entirely sure why some other beauty hadn't snapped him up before. He was not handsome by any stretch of the imagination, but neither was he repulsively ugly. His manners, too, were perfectly fine, if not fascinating.

Nor, for that matter, could she understand why he'd chosen to fix his attentions on her. Apparently, Cynthia and Blanche thought exactly the same.

"Thank you, Mr Bates," Prudy said, trying for a coy smile. She had to be careful with coy looks and glances. She was pretty enough, but not ravishingly beautiful like Catherine. Besides her sister, she tended to look plain, but there wasn't a great deal she could do about that.

Prudy had plenty of *good features* – that was what people said when you weren't particularly pretty – but none of them were outstanding. She had nice hair, dark brown, shot through with lights of gold, red, and chestnut, just like Catherine's hair. She had a round face and full lips, which would cover her ever-so-slightly protruding front teeth if she was careful. Catherine had said once that Prudy looked like a sweet little rabbit.

Prudy wasn't sure she could consider that a compliment.

Aside from that, she had entirely dull sand-coloured eyes, nothing like Catherine's mysterious blue-green ones.

Still, it could not be helped, and Prudy was contented enough with her own face.

"Would you like to dance, Miss Prudence?" Isaac managed at last, as Prudy knew he would.

"I should love that, Mr Bates," she responded, getting up at once, ignoring Cynthia's sniggers. They could laugh all they wanted. Mr Bates had asked *her* to dance, not them.

Isaac took her hand in one of his, large and too well-calloused for a proper gentleman's hand, and led her onto the dance floor for the next set.

Frankly, Prudy was relieved. The night had gone by quickly, and she hadn't danced more than a handful of dances. Her father was sure to ask, and he was never pleased to think that his girls had sat in the corner all evening – like a poor little wallflower of a church mouse, he was fond of saying – and there would be lectures.

Besides, Prudy wanted to dance. Her feet had been twitching to the music for the past hour or so.

The music began, the dancers bowed to each other, and they started to dance.

For a minute or two, Prudy and Isaac skipped and jogged around in each other in silence, but soon enough the dance slowed down a little. She could almost see Isaac's thoughts whirring, trying to think of something interesting to say, something to hold her attention.

"Miss Copperwell's dress is exceptionally beautiful," he said, then his eyes widened. "Not... not that yours is *not*, Miss Prudence, I only meant..."

"Please, you won't offend me by complimenting my older sister," Prudy laughed. "She's remarkably beautiful, is she not? I'm tremendously proud of her. I can say with truth that she's my closest friend."

Isaac relaxed a little. "This is one thing I like very much about you, Miss Prudence. Nothing seems to concern you at all. You are always light and happy, always entertaining."

"Well, one does one's best."

The dance continued for a few more minutes.

Prudy had, of course, considered marrying Isaac Bates. Any woman pursued by a man of such good fortune would think about trying to catch him, and it would make her father very proud. It would be good for Catherine, too. If Prudy made a good marriage, then perhaps Catherine would... well, enough said on that matter.

She had, however, rejected the idea. Isaac Bates was pleasant enough, but Prudy felt no more drawn to him than... well, than she felt *drawn to* her father. She felt, in a strange, visceral sort of way, that she could not fall in love with him, no matter how much she tried. Really, then, it wasn't fair on either of them.

"You have so many friends, too, Miss Prudence," Isaac continued. "You are remarkably popular."

"Well, I suppose so. I never really thought of it. I do have many acquaintances, it's true."

"I am not a man who makes friends easily, myself. I admire it in others."

Prudy mentally reviewed her friends and acquaintances, thinking of something to say about one of them. Nothing particular sprang to mind, so she decided to concentrate instead on the dance, and let silence fall again.

Then she spotted her father on the edge of the crowd, and her steps faltered.

He was standing in a secluded corner by the mantelpiece, speaking to a man wearing the finest, most expensive-looking coat Prudy had ever seen, all gold trimming and red velvet, covering his wide back neatly.

However, it was her father's expression which made her nearly miss a beat.

Mr Jasper Copperwell never smiled much at the best of times, but now his expression was... well, one might call it *grim*. Worried, even.

A kernel of worry unfurled itself in Prudy's chest. Isaac took her hand for the promenading, and she was obliged to turn away from her father and concentrate on dancing.

The final few minutes dragged, but at long last the dance ended with a triumphant flourish, and the dancers laughed and clapped, bowing to each other.

"Miss Prudence, I wonder if I could bother you for another..." Isaac began, but Prudy cut him off, a little too rudely for dealing with such a gentleman.

"Do excuse me, Mr Bates, I must see to my father," she said in a rush, not stopping to hear Isaac mumble an agreement before she hurried off into the crowd.

Jasper Copperwell was alone by the time Prudy reached him, leaning against the mantelpiece, swilling amber liquid about in a brandy glass. The man was tall, rake-thin, and stood ramrod straight from the posture lessons he'd received as a child, which judging from the stories he told had almost broken his spine. He was pale, with a long nose, and the same sand-coloured eyes he'd

9

bequeathed to his younger daughter. He was around forty years of age but could be taken for older.

He was, of course, frowning. He glanced down at Prudy, pushing breathlessly towards him, and his frown deepened.

"What do you want, Prudence? I saw you dancing with Isaac Bates. Why not go back and talk to him?"

"Where's that man you were talking to?"

Jasper blinked. "What man?"

"The man in the red velvet and gold coat."

Jasper scowled. "Oh. Him."

"Who was he?"

"The Marquess."

"Who?"

"It's none of your business, girl. Haven't you people to talk to?"

Prudy flinched, fighting to hold her composure. Tears stung at her eyes, and she hated that. It was humiliating how easily her father's sharp words could make her want to cry. Really, she ought to be used to it by now.

"I just wondered," she mumbled.

"Hmph. A little less curiosity and a little more initiative is in order, I think. For now, go fetch your sister and mother. We're leaving soon."

He drained his brandy glass, set it down with a *clack*, and then walked over without another word or a backwards glance.

Sighing, Prudy turned around to look for her family. Catherine was where she had left her. Mrs Lydia Copperwell was in the same place she'd sat all evening – the matrons' chairs along the wall, sitting stooped-over, faded, and thoroughly bored. It would be no hard thing to round *her* up. She'd been beautiful once, like Catherine, but years of boredom and lack of attention had turned her into a drooping, faded old flower, with not much to say and only the memories of her beauty to sustain her.

Prudy pointedly turned away from her mother. She would go and find Catherine first.

***

"I thought Papa said he was leaving?" Catherine remarked,

pulling her shawl tighter around herself.

The night was well along. In fact, it was close to one in the morning by now. The two Copperwell girls were waiting in the carriage, their breaths frosting in clouds in front of them, waiting for their parents to join them so they could all leave.

Isaac Bates had tried several times to get close to Prudy, apparently to say goodbye, but really, she couldn't be bothered. She'd see him again, no doubt. It was called the last ball of the Season, but there would always be more social events.

"What is *taking* them so long?" Prudy muttered, leaning forward. "I want to go to bed. It's freezing out here. These gowns aren't built for being outside in the winter, and the shawls are next to useless."

"I'm seeing him tomorrow," Catherine said, in a rush.

There was a brief silence between them.

"Seeing who?" Prudy hazarded, and her sister rolled her eyes.

"Who do you think? *Simon*."

Prudy bit her lower lip hard. "I wish you'd be careful, Catherine."

"Of course I'm careful. Why, don't you like Simon?"

Prudy sighed. Simon Gardener was, ironically, a tailor.

No, not even a tailor. A tailor's *apprentice*. They'd met him at a modiste's, run by one of the fashionable faux-French women who operated in Derby, and Simon had stood out a mile.

For one thing, he was remarkably handsome. He had sandy-blond hair, thick and curling, brushed neatly back from a square, well-shaped faced, saved from the blunt lines of ugly masculinity by a beautiful smile, a swooping nose, and a pair of large, chocolate-brown eyes framed by long, black lashes that most of the ladies in London would kill for.

He had helped adjust one of Prudy's gowns, and she'd found him pleasant, likeable, and hard-working.

Catherine, however, had been blown away. Prudy had seen it the second they looked at each other. For his part, Simon had almost staggered, looking ready to faint.

She'd thought no more of it until, a month or so later, Catherine confessed to meeting Simon in secret, walking out together in places where they would not be spotted.

11

This was, naturally, a problem.

"I like Simon very much," Prudy admitted. "He loves you deeply, that's very clear. But think of the practicalities. For one thing, he doesn't have any money, and neither do you."

"I have money."

"You have the money Papa will settle on you when you marry," Prudy countered. "I don't think he'll let you have it if you marry a tailor."

Catherine sighed. "Please, Prudy, don't you turn against me. With Simon around, I... I feel like I'm *living* for the first time in my life. Like I've been holding my breath forever, and now I can *breathe*."

Prudy leaned forward, taking her sister's hand. "I'm not turning against you, truly I'm not. I just... I just don't want you to end up packed off to Bath, like poor Lady Penelope. Or chased by a monster, for that matter."

"I thought you didn't believe in monsters."

"I don't. But I believe in what Society does to ladies who don't toe the line. Catherine, you must be so, so careful."

"I know what I'm doing, Prudy," Catherine said, giving her sister's hand a quick squeeze. "Don't worry about me."

"I can't help it," Prudy sighed. She could see their parents approaching now. Jasper strode ahead, unsmiling, head down. Lydia scuttled behind him, trying and failing to keep up with her husband's long strides. As for Jasper, he probably would not have noticed if he had left his wife back in the ballroom.

"They're coming," Prudy added, as a hint for Catherine to stop talking about Simon.

Their parents did not, needless to say, know that Catherine was in love with a tailor's apprentice.

"It's so wonderful," Catherine murmured. "Being in love, I mean. I had an idea that it was all pain and suffering, but really, it isn't."

"I'll have to take your word for it."

Catherine threw a quick smile at her, teeth glittering in the moonlight. "Oh, just wait till you fall in love, Prudy. You'll go head over heels, and you'll know exactly what I'm talking about."

Prudy snorted, picking non-existent bits of fluff off her skirts. Love was that elusive, intoxicating things that young women whispered about in corners, searching the pages of novels and poetry books for clues as to where to find it. In Prudy's opinion, the whole business was a ploy to trick women into marriage.

It was infuriating, therefore, that she still longed for it with every fibre of her being.

"Oh, I think not, Catherine," she answered smoothly. "I think not."

Chapter Two

Home at last. My feet are so sore I think they might fall off.

Prudy toed off her dancing slippers with a sigh of relief. Her sore toes were mostly due to the pinching, unforgiving shoes than from too much dancing. Some famous beauties were said to have danced through a pair of slippers every night at a ball, but Prudy had never had that problem. She wasn't asked to dance enough, and of course a lady couldn't dance with a gentleman more than once, not if you didn't want people to *talk*.

It was infuriating, really. Prudy had made a friend earlier in the Season, a lisping young dandy of twenty who seemed far more interested in the company of gentlemen than he did of ladies, and Prudy had known right away that he wasn't going to propose to her, which was something of a relief. They'd danced together and spent time together at each ball, and he was enormously entertaining.

She'd enjoyed his company and had often thought it a pity that they couldn't dance together often, because Marcus really *was* an excellent dancer.

The friendship had come to a halt after some whispers had reached Jasper's ears, and he'd bluntly informed his daughter that the match would not meet with his approval, and she'd better leave the man alone. Shortly after, Marcus had dropped out of Society after some scandal or another, and Prudy was left friendless again.

Or rather, not friendless, not with Cynthia and Blanche and their pooled acquaintances. If you counted that sort of thing.

The shoes were gone now, kicked into the corner of the room, and Prudy peeled off her gown and let it crumple on the floor. She always told the maids to take themselves to bed on late nights like this – most of them were up at six every morning, and the clock was now inching towards half past one – and left the mess for them to tidy up later. Prudy was just beginning the laborious task of unpinning her hair when she heard voices.

Raised voices.

Who's shouting at this time of the night? She thought, perplexed. Easing open the door, Prudy strained her ears.

14

Jasper was the one shouting, naturally. She could hear him all the way downstairs. A muffled sob came after, and the hairs on the back of her neck prickled. Tucking her robe around her, and entirely forgetting about her half-undone hair, Prudy crept to the top of the staircase.

Jasper's study was near the entrance of the hall and was of course off-limits to everybody except a few select servants, who were allowed in to clean. At the moment, to her surprise, the door stood ajar. A night footman was on duty, standing nervously by the door. He could clearly hear every word. Their eyes met as Prudy began to tiptoe down the stairs, and she lifted one finger to her lips.

"Jasper, please..." Lydia's voice came from the open door, weak and unheeded and immediately spoken over.

"I break my back to get a good match for you, Catherine, and this is the thanks I get?" Jasper thundered, drowning out his wife's fragile voice.

Prudy pressed a hand over her mouth.

Catherine. No.

"I am obliged to you for your care, Papa," Catherine spoke up, her voice broken and choked with tears, "but I can't marry him."

"You don't even know the man!"

"And that is why I cannot..."

"Have you any other matches? No, you do not. Every respectable offer you have received this Season, you have turned down. You won't even entertain any suitable gentlemen. What do you expect me to do? You won't stay pretty forever. Look at your mother!"

Prudy winced, eyes immediately flying to the footman. The man kept his eyes fixed straight ahead, pretending he couldn't hear. It wasn't the first time Prudy wanted to sink with shame over her father's behaviour, and of course it wouldn't be the last.

"I won't marry him, Papa. If the match was only done tonight, then I'm sure it can be undone at once. If you would just..." Catherine broke off with a cry, as if she'd been struck or grabbed, and Prudy flinched, ready to dash across the foyer and into the study. What she would do, exactly, once she got there was anyone's guess.

15

"The Marquess is not a patient man," Jasper said, teeth gritted. "This match is happening. You haven't a penny of your own, my girl, and may I remind you that you are not yet one and twenty. You'll do as I say."

There was a commotion after that, and Catherine came shooting out of the study, hair a mess, still wearing her royal-blue gown from the party. Prudy flinched, pressing herself against the banister as if that would help her go unnoticed. Catherine's eyes were swollen and puffy, cheeks tear-stained, and she rushed past her sister without a second glance.

Catherine hurtled upstairs, and Prudy heard her stamp across the landing and slam her door. Nobody came after her, and Prudy hastily followed, in case one of her parents should come out and catch her eavesdropping.

Casting an apologetic look at the footman – who looked just as miserable as Prudy felt – she hurried back upstairs, heading straight to the lavender-painted door to Catherine's room.

Prudy tapped twice, keeping her voice low. Their parents slept in the opposite wing of the house, so she had no worry of being overheard.

"Catherine? Catherine, let me in."

"The door's not locked," came the weak reply.

Prudy turned the handle and slipped inside.

Catherine's room was the opposite to Prudy's. It was neat, impeccably so, with sober and tasteful decorations. No lamps or candles were lit, and it took her a few moments to adjust her eyes to the darkness.

Catherine was lying on her side on the bed, curled into a ball, facing away from the door. She was sobbing quietly, shoulders heaving.

Prudy wavered in the door for a moment. Wouldn't it be easier to just go to bed? She was so tired, and perhaps Catherine would have recovered by the morning. Surely their father would reconsider. He wouldn't *really* force her to get married. That sort of thing only happened in novels.

Surely.

Prudy shuffled forward, feeling her way across the dark room, and crawled onto the bed beside her sister.

"You heard, I suppose?" Catherine said, voice choked. "The

Marquess of Derby wants a wife for his nephew. The man seldom goes into Society, so it's all going to be arranged quietly. He saw me, and asked Papa for his permission. Papa gave it. The wedding is going ahead."

There was a taut silence. Prudy knew the Marquess of Derby by reputation, at least. A man as powerful as him wouldn't bother himself with the acquaintance of some unmarried little Miss.

"But... but what about Simon? Surely Papa won't make you..." Prudy began weakly, but was interrupted by Catherine sitting bolt upright and spinning around to face her, eyes glittering.

"Oh, stop it, Prudence! You don't understand a thing, do you? Haven't you been saying right from the start that Simon and I could never be together? How did you think this was going to end?"

Prudy recoiled from her sister's livid, tear-stained expression.

"I... I suppose I thought it would just... just stop."

"I'm in love with him, Prudence! It never *just stops*. I can't live without him. I don't care about Papa's money, I never have. It hasn't made Mama happy, has it? We were waiting for Simon to save up enough money, and then maybe..." she trailed off, squeezing her eyes closed. More tears came leaking out, dripping from the edge of her chin. "It's too late now," she murmured, voice ragged.

Catherine flopped down onto the pillows, muffling her sobs. Prudy sat where she was, rigid with shock. She felt sick and shaky, and part of her was terrified that one of their parents would burst in at any moment, raging and shouting and demanding an explanation.

"Are... are you going to run away with him?" Prudy asked, voice shaking.

Catherine shook her head. "I thought about it. It would never work. I don't have a penny, as Papa so kindly said, and Simon has hardly any savings. He would need to leave his work behind, and I daresay Papa would make sure he never got work in Derby again. I'm not qualified for any work at all, besides painting a few slapdash watercolours and a few dull embroidery projects, and without a note of refence, I don't know if Simon could get work, either. There are lots of tailors' apprentices around, ones that

17

haven't ruined their reputations." She sniffed loudly. "I'd ruin him, Prudy. If word got out – and it would get out – nobody would buy so much as a yard of ribbon from him. We'd have nothing. He loves his work, and I can't... I can't take it from him."

"But if he loves you..." Prudy tried, but Catherine rounded on her again.

"Don't be such a child, Prudy! You can't eat love, can you? Love won't put a roof over anyone's head!"

"But... but you said..."

"Forget about what I said," Catherine said dully. Hauling herself into a sitting position, she reached over and lit a candle. "I was stupid."

"You aren't stupid, Catherine."

"Oh, no? Would a clever girl fall in love with a tailor? I'm not rich enough for such nonsense. I'm not rich at all."

The candle gave off a flickering, buttery glow, playing over Catherine's tangled hair and tear-stained face. In that rare moment, Catherine in her misery looked ugly. Her face was red and swollen, blotchy with tears, and her lips dry and bitten. Her gown was rumpled, the expensive lace around the cuffs torn.

Prudy fisted her hands into the sheets.

"We won't let this happen," she said firmly. "Look at me, Catherine. I... I can't say that I approve of Simon and you, for obvious reasons, but I won't stand by and watch you be forced to leave the man you love behind. The business with the Marquess' nephew can be gotten over, I'm sure of it. If you just stand firm..."

"Papa can force me to marry," Catherine said listlessly. "Until I'm twenty-one, I have to abide by his rules. Perhaps he can't literally drag me down the aisle, but by law, I have to obey him. And don't try and say that he would never do something like that, because we both know that he would. He will. He's going to, if I resist. This match with the Marquess' nephew is a good one, and Papa already has his mind set on it. I think he already imagines me married to the man. It'll be a match for everybody in town to talk about, and the wedding will be quiet and inexpensive. The man doesn't like drawing attention, I've been told."

Catherine sniffled, wiping her nose with the back of her hand, and smiled weakly.

"The betrothal notice is going in the *Gazette* as soon as

possible. It's happening, Prudy. There's nothing we can do about it."

"I don't believe that," Prudy responded. To her surprise, anger was welling up inside her.

Anger was not, of course, an appropriate emotion for a lady to feel, under any circumstances. Prudy's finishing school had been very harsh on this point, reminding the girls that they would *never* wish to be considered a *shrew*. Oh, certainly not.

By her estimation, a lady should go through life – the disappointments of love, the harshness and possible cruelties of a husband, the pains of childbirth, and the slow, inevitable decline into irrelevance and invisibility – without experiencing anything stronger than perhaps a mild sensation of discontent.

So long as they did not *pout* or *sulk*, naturally.

There'd been no discussion on what to do about rage, when it boiled up inside one and threatened to choke a lady, like Prudy was feeling right now.

She reached out for her sister's hand, holding it tight.

"We aren't going to let this happen," she said, voice low and furious. "If you love Simon, if you *truly* love him, then we shall move heaven and earth to let you be with him. I promise you that, Catherine. I *will* save you from this."

Catherine eyed her sister for a long moment. Then she began to laugh. It was a dry, mirthless laugh, very unpleasant.

"Oh, Prudy," she murmured, cupping her little sister's cheek with one cold hand. "You're so kind. So sweet. I don't know what I've done to deserve.you. I'm sorry that I was so snappish with you – you didn't deserve that. But there's nothing we can do."

"Of course there is! We could... we could..." Prudy stammered, waiting for some miraculous idea to come popping into her brain, one that would allow everything to go back to the way it was, with the fat Marquess and his awful nephew melting away as if they'd never existed.

Catherine only smiled tiredly, waiting patiently for Prudy to begin to realize that no such idea was coming.

"There you are, you see?" she said, sounding regretful. "I've thought and thought, too, but there's nothing we can do. Unless I'm willing to make myself and the man I love destitute – which I'm not – my only choice is to marry the Marquess' nephew. It's... it's awful, I know, but there are women in worse situations than me. I'll never forget Simon, or how much I loved him, and I hope that with time he'll forget me. Make your peace with this, Prudy, and I'll try to do the same."

She rolled over, turning her back to her sister.

"I can't believe that," Prudy insisted. "There must be something..."

"The wedding will take place in two weeks," Catherine interrupted. "That's plenty of time for us to get used to the idea."

"But..."

"I'm very tired, Prudy. I'd like to go to sleep. Goodnight."

Faced with this dismissal, Prudy had no choice but to creep out of her sister's room and back into her own, into her cold bed.

She didn't sleep much that night.

There must be something, Prudy thought, again and again, like a chant in her mind.

I must be able to do something about this. But what?

Chapter Three

Rycroft Hall

Bartholomew Harrington, Marquess of Derby, sat serenely in a wide armchair and waited for his nephew's rage to burn itself out.

Bartholomew had always been a rather portly man, despite a few years of desperate dieting and corset-wearing in his youth, and his width had grown steadily until now, when at the age of forty-five, he struggled to fit in most chairs.

He didn't particularly care anymore. He'd never been a *marrying* kind of man, and since the good Lord had seen fit to make him plump all his life, there seemed no sense in stopping now.

A lamp which had been considered rather valuable came hurtling past Bartholomew's head, smashing against the wall. He contemplated helping himself to another cup of tea.

"Are you quite finished, Gideon?" he asked.

The other figure in the room had his back turned, shoulders heaving, leaning heavily on his cane. Bartholomew was conscious of a pang of worry – Gideon ought not to exert himself so intensely. Of course, such worrying would only incense his nephew further, so Bartholomew decided not to mention it.

"I don't wish to be married, Uncle," Gideon said, back still turned. "You know that, and you know why."

"I do know it. I didn't take this step lightly, my boy. You're, what? Seven and twenty?"

"Eight and twenty, as well you know."

"Humph. Well, that's *youth*, you know. You'll be Marquess of Derby one day, and it stands to reason that you should marry and procure a few heirs."

Gideon turned, shooting a scornful look over his shoulder. His expression was veiled in the gloom, the thick velvet curtains shutting out most of the light.

"Like you did, Uncle? From what I remember, you preferred the company of your friends all your life, and were happy enough with that."

"So I did, so I did," Bartholomew said comfortably. "And perhaps if *you* had a gaggle of friends, I'd be less worried about you."

"I'm fine."

Well, that was obviously a lie, but Bartholomew had long since learned not to say as much. Sometimes, if he closed his eyes, he could see the bright-faced twenty-one-year-old his nephew had once been, possessed of smooth, pale good looks, pale eyes coupled with black hair and an ethereal way about him that would make any Gothic author swoon.

The boy is gone. Stop it, Bartholomew. Focus on the here and now.

"Miss Catherine Copperwell is an excellent young woman," Bartholomew said firmly. "Do you think I just had the ladies of Derby queued up in a line, and then chose one for you?"

"I wouldn't put it past you," Gideon retorted. "You've never had any time for women, have you, Uncle? It was remarked on often, when you were younger."

There was a heartbeat of silence.

"That," Bartholomew said quietly, "was not a kind thing to say."

Gideon's narrow shoulders sagged.

"I'm sorry," he said, voice barely louder than a whisper. "I'm sorry, Uncle. I never meant..."

"It's quite alright, my boy. I'm not upset. This news is a shock, I understand. Now, you can make amends by sitting down and pouring us both a cup of tea."

Gideon obeyed, clumping silently across the room. He sat down into the chair opposite, leaning his silver-tipped cane against the arm of the chair. For a moment or two, there was silence, broken only by the gentle trickle of tea landing in teacups, the slop of milk, and the regular splash of Bartholomew's usual four sugars being added to his own cup.

"As I said, I chose Miss Copperwell very carefully," Bartholomew continued. Most of Gideon's rage – which was mostly made up of panic and frustration, of course – had melted away, leaving him exhausted. "She's a very suitable young woman, a very nice girl, and I think you will like her."

"Do you think she'll like me?"

"She is a nice girl," Bartholomew repeated. "Her father assured me that her affections are not engaged elsewhere, and since the Season is ending, it's fair to assume that she would have remained unmarried for another half-year at least."

He had spent a few weeks in Society observing the eligible young ladies in town. Most of them were pretty, and were considered *accomplished*, but that hardly meant anything. He wanted a pretty girl, for Gideon's sake, but naturally she would have to be much more than that. Money was irrelevant, and indeed Miss Copperwell's dowry was nothing compared to the money Bartholomew had, and the money Gideon would one day inherit.

Miss Copperwell was strikingly pretty, easily the most beautiful girl in town, but Bartholomew had noticed other qualities in her, too. She was exceptionally kind, very charming without being false, and was well-spoken of by all but the most jealous of her peers. Miss Copperwell was not a flirt, was not a gossip, and seemed to be remarkably confident in herself and her beliefs.

Another thing he had noticed was Miss Copperwell's relationship with her sister. Miss Prudence, the younger Copperwell girl, was a good-natured creature, rather a sharp gossip but not exactly unkind, and unfortunately plain beside her beautiful sister. However, the two girls obviously adored each other, and Miss Prudence had never shown anything but adoration towards Miss Copperwell.

That was good. Bartholomew had often noticed that sibling relationships could tell a great deal about a person. If Miss Copperwell's sister adored her, he could be sure that she would not end up a cruel, overbearing fool like her father, or a husk like her mother. He had been taken by Miss Copperwell and her qualities almost at once, and the new few weeks had only strengthened his beliefs that the girl was perfect to become Lady Rycroft, his nephew's wife.

"You'll like her," Bartholomew assured him, taking a sip of his tea. "Why don't you open those wretched curtains, Gideon? This study is a nice-looking room, but one can never *see* it because it's so dark in here."

"Perhaps I like the dark, Uncle. It suits me. Besides, that waistcoat you're wearing is already giving me a headache. If the

23

sun shone in and hit those gilt buttons, it would blind us both."

"Humph. If you're trying to hide the fact that Agatha hasn't dusted in here in goodness only knows how long, it's not working. I can smell the dust."

Gideon bridled at that. "Agatha is not getting any younger, and she works hard enough. And don't change the subject, please. You know quite well that I don't wish to be married, so why are you insisting on it?"

"You know why. I've said it a thousand times. You'll inherit my position and my estate, and what then? If you insist on your life of seclusion, there's nothing I can do about that, but I will *not* see my estate rot away after your death because you never bothered to have an heir. I won't see it entailed to some distant fool who doesn't know how to be a gentleman."

"Well, considering that I won't inherit the place at all till after your death, I think it's fair to say that you won't see any of that." Gideon pointed out.

Bartholomew snorted. "Oh, very funny, I'm sure."

It was hard to tell in the dark, but he was sure that his nephew smiled, even just a little. Progress, then.

"I don't wish to share my life with anyone, Uncle."

Perhaps not.

Bartholomew sighed, heaving his bulk forward to place his cup back on the table.

"You don't *need* to share your life with the girl. Marriage is a business affair, at the end of the day. This is a large house, and you don't need to see her. She might even want to go to London, or back to Derby, and live an entirely separate life."

"While you are painting a truly lovely portrait of marriage, Uncle, I'd like to point out that you wanted me to get heirs."

"Well, yes. You will need to produce at least *one* heir. A boy, preferably. But that will require very little effort on your part, you know."

Gideon leaned forward, smiling mirthlessly. "And what about my wife, Uncle? What about on our wedding night, when she realizes that her husband is a scarred ghost, rotting from the outside in? I'm not entirely sure there's anything left of me at all, beneath the skin."

"Nonsense," Bartholomew said, sharper than he intended.

"She's a proper, chaste little thing, and won't have a clue. You can always blow out the candles."

"Oh, very nice, Uncle, very nice indeed. You know that she'll have to see me before we marry, at least for a minute or two? Or would you rather I wear a heavy black veil when we say our vows?"

He sniffed. "You've been reading too many novels. It isn't… isn't that bad, you know."

It was a hollow lie, and they both knew it. Gideon looked away, and Bartholomew picked at his gold cufflinks, wishing he could have sounded more convincing.

"This is a mistake," Gideon said at last. "I know you mean well, Uncle, and I know you care about me. But I can't agree to this. I am sorry. I hope Miss Copperwell is not disappointed, although I think that if she could see me in person, she'd consider herself lucky to have escaped."

Bartholomew drew in a ragged sigh. He was exhausted and getting far too old for this nonsense.

I wish it hadn't come to this.

"I command you to marry her, Gideon."

As expected, his nephew only raised thin black brows at him.

"I beg your pardon? I'm not a dog, Uncle. I don't sit and stay on command."

"No need to tell me twice. If you marry her, I'll double your allowance. If you produce a child, I'll *triple* it."

Gideon actually gave a low chuckle at that. "You should know me better than that. I don't care for money. What I have is sufficient."

Bartholomew shifted in his seat, working himself up for the next thing he had to say.

"Very well. If you do not oblige me in this, I'll cut you off entirely."

The smile disappeared from Gideon's face.

"Fine. Cut me off, then. I don't care. I don't have a great deal of expenses, you know."

"Perhaps not," Bartholomew acknowledged. "But you won't be able to pay Joseph and Agatha's wages."

That was a low blow. Gideon flinched as if he'd been slapped.

"That's not fair."

25

No, Bartholomew thought unhappily. *It's not.*

He pressed on, nevertheless, because he'd had a great deal of time to think about how to manage Gideon, about this last-ditch attempt to bring back the cheerful, happy young nephew he'd once had.

"It would be a pity," he said, inspecting his nails. "As you said earlier, neither of them is getting any younger. In their youth, I believe both of them had opportunities to take on well-paying jobs elsewhere. Of course, they chose to stay here. With you. But if I were to cut you off, you would not be able to pay them. I daresay they'd try to stay as long as they could, running through their savings, but soon enough they would have no choice but to leave. Goodness only knows what would await them if they ventured out into the world. I would remind you too that their pensions are my expense, held at my discretion. The world is not kind to people of their age, and..."

"Enough," Gideon interrupted crisply. He hauled himself to his feet, leaning heavily on his cane, and made his way over to the large desk in the corner of the room, piled with books and papers. For a moment, Bartholomew half expected to have something else thrown at him. He would have deserved it, really.

Guilt bubbling in his chest, Bartholomew conjured up an image of Agatha Moss and Joseph Smith, both well into their fifties, constantly bickering, always cheerful, always able to wring a half smile at the very least out of Gideon. It was wrong of him to threaten them, but if Gideon would not listen...

"If you like this Miss Copperwell so much," Gideon stated at last, "I'm surprised you want to condemn her to a life with me."

"Oh, Gideon, please do stop this. I've tried my best to... to bring you back, but nothing works. This is the last thing I can think of."

"What, forcing me into a marriage? I think you should go."

"Not before you give me your word that you'll go along with this. The war has been over for seven years, Gideon."

In the poor light, Bartholomew saw Gideon squeeze his eyes closed, swaying ever so slightly where he stood.

"It'll never be over for me, though," he murmured, so quietly that Bartholomew wasn't sure whether he meant to be heard.

He waited, though, not moving from the armchair. Gideon

heaved a sigh, passing a hand over his face.

"I have no choice to agree, then," he said flatly, not meeting his uncle's eye. "I condemn Miss Copperwell and myself to a life of misery. A life for a life, I suppose. Ours for Agatha and Joseph's."

Bartholomew smothered a sigh of relief. He had no idea what he would have done had his nephew called his bluff.

No need to worry about it, now.

"I'm glad you've made this decision, my boy," Bartholomew said, heaving himself to his feet.

Gideon gave a short laugh. "Not much of a decision, was it? Not much of a choice."

"Don't be like that. I have it on good authority that marriage makes men very happy."

"I'll be sure to mention that to Miss Copperwell, when she's blubbering her way through her vows."

"That's the spirit. Now, you and I will go to the Copperwells' home in two weeks' time, to meet the young lady and iron out any details regarding the wedding."

He saw the colour drain out of Gideon's face, if indeed there was any colour already *in* his face to drain away. Indeed, that man needed to see the sun every once in a while.

"Oh, nice," Gideon snapped. "A *wedding*. How fun. You know how I've always dreamed of one."

"Sarcasm does not become you, Gideon. The wedding will be a quiet affair – Mr Copperwell was more than happy to choose a cheap ceremony – and you can forgo the wedding breakfast if you prefer, and simply have your bride join you at home."

That seemed to ease Gideon's worries, at least a little. The young man nibbled his lower lip, eyes crinkling with dread, the sort of dread a man of eight-and-twenty shouldn't be feeling.

Bartholomew reminded himself that Gideon was no ordinary young man. Not after what he'd seen, what he'd done, what he'd experienced.

"I will leave you now," Bartholomew said heavily, glancing at the congealing cake set out on the tea-tray. Neither of them had touched it. For one of them, this was very much out of character.

Gideon nodded wordlessly. He didn't bother to try and escort his uncle out, and Bartholomew didn't ask for it.

Outside, ready to climb into his carriage – Bartholomew

paused to glance up at the crumbling old manor, coated with moss and worn down by time. As he'd expected, Gideon was standing at the window of his study, watching him. He lifted a pallid hand in farewell, and Bartholomew waved back.

I'm sorry, my boy, he thought miserably. *It was for the best. Please, please believe me.*

Then he climbed heavily into his carriage and drove away.

Chapter Four

Two Weeks Later, The Copperwell Estate

"For the last time, Prudence," Lydia Copperwell said, more sharply than she could usually manage, "sit down and be still!"

Prudy unwillingly dropped into her seat. Her sewing lay beside her, but she made no move to pick it up. She wasn't sure she could even concentrate on the newest Mrs Radcliffe novel, which she had been waiting for with bated breath for months now, keen to borrow it from the circulating library.

"What if Catherine really, *truly* cannot stand him?" she tried again.

Lydia glowered at her. "Catherine will do her duty. Won't you?"

"Yes, Mama," Catherine answered listlessly.

She hadn't looked well lately. Her bloom had gone, her eyes blank, and her hair had lost its gloss. She didn't bother to choose fine dresses like she had before, just putting on whatever the maids recommended. Prudy had seen the way their father eyed her over the dinner table, anxious and annoyed.

Today, he'd insisted on her putting on a brand-new dress, in satin so pink it looked as though you could eat it, with rubies to match. Catherine had obediently pulled on the dress, but it hung limply from her frame. Everything about her shouted *misery*.

Maybe when her so-called fiancé sees her, he'll change his mind, Prudy thought. *Maybe he'll take pity on her.*

Frankly, that seemed unlikely. Catherine had neatly stopped any of Prudy's attempts to talk about the matter, but of course that hadn't stopped her enterprising little sister from researching the man in question.

Lord Gideon Rycroft was in his late twenties, and Prudy had not been able to unearth anything good about him.

"Do you know, he survived the war when his whole platoon died?" Prudy commented, after a long pause. "They say he killed hundreds – no, *thousands* of men in France. He hasn't been seen for years, *and* they say that Rycroft Manor is haunted, and Dalton woods inhabited by a monster."

Lydia shot a poisonous look at her youngest daughter. "Hold your tongue, Prudence."

Prudy ignored her. She hadn't been in the habit of listening to her mother for years, and she had no intention of starting now.

"He could be a monster, and we'd never know," she added. "Cynthia said that her maid, Madeline, says that he only eats meat, and his teeth are…"

"Prudy, please stop."

That was Catherine. Prudy glanced at her sister and saw that she was white and shaking. A knot of guilt tightened in her chest.

"I'm sorry," Prudy murmured. Nobody responded.

Silence descended again, broken only by the quite whisper of Lydia's needle as it pulled through, trailing blood-red embroidery thread, and the regular ticking of the clock in the corner. Catherine stared into space, her book hanging unheeded from her fingers. She hadn't turned a page in the last hour or so.

Prudy wanted desperately to get up and pace, to *do* something, but that sort of fidgeting would drive her mother wild and would bother Catherine.

There must be something I can do. Anything. Anything!

An idea was beginning to take shape in her head, but it felt more like wild imaginings than anything real. It was too silly even to consider. They'd laugh at her. They'd all laugh at her, and her father would be so angry, and Catherine so humiliated…

Catherine. Prudy closed her eyes.

She'd tried to talk to her father, of course, without saying anything about Simon. He'd dismissed her at once, the instant the words *perhaps it's not the right match for Catherine* had crossed her lips. And then none of them had seen him for at least a week, as he closeted himself away to make the arrangements for the wedding.

As far as Prudy knew, Catherine had not seen Simon at all. Perhaps she'd sent him a note or a letter, but if she had not, he wouldn't know about it. Perhaps her courage had given out, and she was just going to stay silent and let him find out by means of gossip, once she was married.

No, that didn't sound like Catherine. Prudy glanced at her sister, her face bone-white and set, and clenched her jaw.

This isn't fair.

30

"Catherine..." Prudy began, leaning towards her sister and ignoring the furious look her mother sent her, but she got no further than that. At that instant, they all heard it – the crunch of carriage wheels on the raked gravel of the drive.

The three of them flew to the window, embroidery and half-read books forgotten.

Sure enough, a large, impressive-looking carriage was making its ponderous way up the drive. It was drawn by *four* horses, had recently been lacquered, and bore an impressive coat of arms on the side. It slowed to a halt in front of the stone steps outside, and they watched in silence as the Marquess of Derby heaved his bulk slowly out of the carriage.

Before they could see the second man, his nephew, Jasper came stamping into the room, flushed red with panic, smoothing his waistcoat down with shaking hands.

"Get away from the window, all of you!" he barked, and was instantly obeyed. "You don't want to let him catch you gawping down at him like ill-bred peasants. Sit down, you fools."

Hypocritically, he lingered at the window himself, watching with pursed lips.

Prudy settled down in the same seat as before, besides her sister. She smoothed out her skirts and cleared her throat.

The idea was throbbing inside her skull now, demanding to be listened to.

It would work, she realized, stomach dropping out from inside her. *It really would work.*

"Papa," she said carefully, keeping her voice genteel and well-modulated. "I was wondering if..."

"What are you doing here, Prudence?" Jasper barked, pausing to inspect his own reflection. "This is an important meeting. Go out into the garden or back to your room, you don't need to be here."

"I want her here," Catherine spoke up instantly. She reached out, taking Prudy's hot little hand in her cold one.

Jasper scowled at his daughters through the reflection.

"Very well, very well. Prudence, go and sit on the footstool by your mother's chair, nobody will notice you there. And Catherine, pinch your cheeks, do *something* to put some colour in your face."

31

Prudy obediently got up and moved to the low footstool, where she'd been obliged to sit as a child, humiliation ringing her ears. Her idea seemed stupid now, and it wouldn't be listened to in any case.

They all flinched at the sound of the door opening. Jasper sucked in a ragged breath and hurried out into the hallway to greet their guests, leaving his womenfolk alone.

Catherine caught her eye across the room and smiled weakly.

"Thank you for trying," she said quietly. "I won't forget how hard you tried."

A lump rose to Prudy's throat.

I must do something.

Then footsteps and voices were echoing along the hallway, and the parlour door inched open. The three women rose simultaneously, angled to meet their fate.

Jasper stepped in first, face flushed, an ingratiating smile on his face. The Marquess followed next, wearing an eye-stinging suit of yellow velvet and a blue-and-red waistcoat to match. He looked thoroughly bored, and barely bowed in response to the ladies' deep curtsies.

Then came Lord Rycroft.

It was only once he stepped into the room that Prudy realized she'd been expecting a young version of the Marquess – plump, confident, and finely dressed. Instead, the man who stepped into the room was slim, narrow-shouldered, no taller than average, and dressed almost entirely in black. Only a deep brown waistcoat and a ruby cravat pin nestled in the folds of bright white linen at his neck indicated that he was not, in fact, in the deepest mourning.

Lord Rycroft was very pale, so pale that she could see a few blue veins running underneath. His face was oval, with a long, swooping nose that gave him an almost pixie-like look, belied by a sharp jaw, and a set of firm black brows. His hair was black and cut neatly, if not fashionably, swept back and kept short at the nape of his neck. He had very pale eyes, blue or green, she wasn't sure, and he rested on a long black cane, tipped with silver. His hands, she noticed, were as pale, slim, and elegant as the rest of him, resting on the top of his cane. He favoured one leg more than another, and she suspected he would walk with a limp.

In short, he was remarkably handsome, although not in the healthy, blond way that Simon was handsome. Prudy glanced at her sister. She wasn't even looking at the man, but at some spot between his face and the floor.

Lydia stepped forward to welcome them, gesturing for them to sit. The Marquess sat heavily down on a sofa, leaving his nephew to perch uncomfortably at the edge of an armchair.

Lord Rycroft's pale eyes swept around the room, seeming to miss no detail. That gaze landed on Prudy, just a moment, then moved on. He did not smile, even when Lydia gave him her hand and effusively welcomed him to their home.

When he turned his head, though, Prudy noticed a few odd pockmarks on the side of his neck, climbing up from his high collar towards his ear, ending just at the line of his jaw. There were a few matching marks on his cheek, but one could only notice them when the light shone.

Glancing at her sister as they sank back down into their respective places, Prudy felt like crying. Catherine's jaw was clenched, no doubt to stop herself from crying.

Don't cry, sister, Prudy thought. *I won't let you marry the Rycroft ghost.*

***

It was mortifying. Of course it was mortifying. Gideon had known from the moment his uncle told him about the plan that coming here would be nothing but humiliation and nonsense.

On the carriage ride here, Bartholomew had made a joke about tempting his 'vampire bat of a nephew' out of his lair. Gideon had begged him not to repeat it. His uncle had obliged, although it seemed to physically pain him to hold back what he clearly thought was an excellent joke.

The rest of them were as he suspected. Mr Copperwell was a grinning sycophant, clearly hoping to curry favour with the Marquess of Derby, even if he was momentarily taken aback by Gideon's thin, pale appearance. There'd been much bowing and many compliments, not one of which was sincere.

Mrs Copperwell seemed kind enough, but hollowed out, like

33

Bartholomew had warned him. The house was large, very fine, a touch pretentious.

That brought him to the two girls. They were both pretty, one in a pink dress which seemed to drain her colour, one in a pale grey gown, seated at her mother's feet and almost tucked away behind her skirts. He guessed which one was Miss Copperwell – the thoroughly miserable one in the pink dress.

His heart sank. She couldn't even look him in the eye. The one in grey, the younger one, was staring at him sure enough, but her face had gone red, probably with horror.

Gideon gripped the top of his cane until the smooth silver dug into his palms.

"Such an honour to have an esteemed captain in our midst," Jasper Copperwell was saying now, much to Gideon's annoyance. "A true war hero. I do hope you can favour us with a few amusing tales from your travels."

"The most amusing thing about war is that foolish ladies and gentlemen seem to think that it's *heroic*," Gideon snapped, before he could stop himself.

It was pointless to hope that Mr Copperwell didn't understand his meaning. The man flushed red to the roots of his hair, and Bartholomew shot Gideon an unamused look. Gideon bit his lip, hard.

In the silence, there was a small, smothered sound. To his amazement, Gideon realized that the younger girl, the one in grey, was trying not to laugh.

Is she laughing at me? No, at her father. She's laughing because I made her father look like a fool. What a charming girl.

He pressed his lips together and avoided her gaze.

Mr Copperwell cleared his throat, recovering.

"Ah, yes, indeed. Tell me, Lord Rycroft, what is your estate like? My daughter has been peppering me with questions about it."

Liar, Gideon thought.

It wasn't polite to say so, naturally, so he cleared his throat and tried to think of something sensible to say.

"It's very large," he managed.

There was a heartbeat of silence, during which he realized to his chagrin that he was expected to say more.

Bartholomew spoke up.

34

"It's a very pleasant house, with plenty of land around it," he said firmly. "As my nephew said, very large. I'd say it's in need of decorating, but there would be plenty of money for Miss Copperwell to do the house up exactly as she likes. I believe young ladies like projects, is that right?"

Miss Copperwell favoured him with the tiniest of smiles. "That would be nice."

Gideon felt a stab of pity for the poor girl. She wasn't even pretending not to be miserable.

What do young women like? Young people in general, maybe? He racked his brain, conjuring up an image of his mother, many years ago, a very active lady who'd liked to ride every morning.

"I have stables," he heard himself say, "and plenty of land for horse riding."

Miss Copperwell gave him a polite smile. "That sounds wonderful, Lord Rycroft."

Perhaps he might have believed her, if the youngest girl hadn't snorted and spoken up.

"Catherine hates riding. She's afraid of horses."

There was a heartbeat of tense silence. Mr Copperwell looked as though he wanted to strangle his own daughter. Miss Copperwell had the grace to look embarrassed at being caught in a lie.

Gideon glanced at his uncle, to find that the man was holding back a smile with difficulty.

"This is my youngest daughter, Prudence, who has not yet learned to imitate her namesake," Mr Copperwell said, voice simmering with anger. "There's no need for her to be here. Prudence, go to your room. We'll speak later."

The girl flushed, but held her ground, curling her fingers around the stool she sat on as if she were afraid of being wrenched up and thrown out.

"There's no need for that," Gideon heard himself say.

Mr Copperwell looked as though he were going to explode.

"As you say, then," he managed, gaze boring into his youngest daughter. The girl met his gaze steadily.

She's getting ready for something, Gideon thought, a tendril of interest uncurling inside him.

35

"I have something to say, actually," Miss Prudence said, voice wobbling.

Mr Copperwell's eyes bulged. "I think not, my girl. In fact..."

"Come now, Jasper," Bartholomew interrupted. "It's not polite to contradict a lady, certainly not one's own daughter. Speak up, Miss Prudence. We are all listening."

Miss Prudence seemed to be unsure whether that was a threat or a reassurance. Clearing her throat, she rose to her feet, stepping into the middle of her room. She met Gideon's eye squarely.

"I do not believe," she began, hesitant but determined, "That my sister will thrive in Rycroft Hall."

"Prudence..." Miss Copperwell began quietly, but her sister did not look at her.

"Since this whole business is a matter of... well, business," Miss Prudence ploughed on, "Perhaps we could renegotiate."

Gideon glanced Bartholomew, who was frowning heavily. His uncle opened his mouth to speak, but Gideon hastily intervened.

This was his life, was it not? It didn't feel like much of a life, but it was *his*, so why should he not manage it himself?

"Go on," he said shortly. "I didn't manage the negotiations myself, and I imagine that Miss Copperwill did not, either. I'm listening."

Miss Prudence let out a long, slow breath, shooting one nervous glance at her father's thunderous face. He guessed that she hadn't expected to get this far.

Still, he found himself interested to see what she was going to say next.

"You're going to propose another candidate for the role of Lady Rycroft?" he prompted, not quite able to hold back a mirthless smile.

"Yes, I am," Miss Prudence huffed. "Why not me?"

There was a moment of silence, then chaos broke out.

"I cannot apologise enough, my lords..." Mr Copperwell was choking out, while his wife pressed her hands to her mouth and moaned aloud. Miss Copperwell was on her feet, tugging at her sister's arm, whispering urgently in her ear. Throughout it all, Miss Prudence held Gideon's eye unblinkingly.

That's right, he thought wryly. *Fight over who gets to*

sacrifice themselves to the beast.

"Well, that seems… I mean, it…" Bartholomew stammered, and really it *was* nice to see his chatty uncle for once lost for words. "Why would you suggest such a thing?"

"There's no denying that the position of Lady Rycroft is a great one," Miss Prudence said smoothly, and now she seemed to be gaining confidence. "But, as I said, I don't think my sister would thrive there. My dowry will be the same as hers, and since it *is* a marriage of convenience and not a love match, it couldn't possibly matter to you, Lord Rycroft, which of us you marry."

She met his eye unflinchingly, and he lifted an eyebrow.

"No," he said flatly. "It does not matter."

"Catherine is the prettier one," Mrs Copperwell piped up, unhelpfully. She earned herself a furious and mortified glare from her husband.

"Both of these young ladies are equally beautiful," Bartholomew said severely. "And they have many other qualities besides their looks."

"This is not necessary," Mr Copperwell said, rising slowly to his feet. "The arrangement has been made for my *oldest* daughter. It's usual for daughters to marry in order of age, is it not? Prudence, I think you are getting above yourself. Catherine, you want to marry Lord Rycroft, do you not?"

The oldest Copperwell girl dropped her eyes. "I will do my duty, Papa," she said flatly.

How very tempting, Gideon thought sourly. *I am duty, nothing more.*

He glanced at Prudence again, narrowing his eyes. There had to be more than this. The younger girl was trying so hard to save her sister – and from what? Not just from him, surely.

Or so you hope.

"What would happen, then, if I were to accept your suggestion?" Gideon asked slowly.

The girl breathed out slowly. "Well, the wedding would go ahead on the same timeline, only with me as your bride instead of my sister. You'd receive my dowry, which will be the same as Catherine would get. And I quite like riding," she added, and Gideon had to suppress a smile at that.

"And what else?"

37

She hesitated, glancing between her sister and her father. "Well, since I would have made such an excellent match, married to your good self, sir, I'm sure that my father would have no need to think of a great match for Catherine. After all, he loves us, his daughters, so very much, he would be happy to see Catherine marry whoever she likes, once I was so well settled."

Bartholomew eyed Mr Copperwell until he turned red and muttered an agreement.

There was a taut pause after that.

Aha, Gideon thought. *He we are at last. The older Copperwell girl has her eye on somebody, and her younger sister wants to keep her free. If her father said she didn't have anybody, then there's a good chance that he doesn't even know.*

"I see," he said aloud.

More silence. Miss Prudence shifted from foot to foot, looking uneasy.

Regretting your decision? He wanted to ask. He didn't. Perhaps the girl was only now starting to realize what would happen to her if he said no. Her father looked like he wanted to kill her, for a start.

"Well?" she said, after a pause. "What do you say, Lord Rycroft? Would you like to marry me instead?"

That sort of bald, straightforward offer was anathema to most Society ladies. Most would swoon in shock at the very notion of it, of *asking a man to marry them* when their Society did not permit women to ask men to dance.

It was refreshing, really. And she made an excellent point – it really did not make a difference. No need for Catherine Copperwell to lose her love.

"Very well, then," Gideon said aloud. "I'll marry you, Miss Prudence."

The girl in question exhaled tightly, and her sister clapped a hand over her mouth.

Bartholomew struggled to his feet.

"Well, then, now that that's settled," he said heavily, "we had really better be going."

You can say that again, Gideon thought sourly.

38

Chapter Five

Four Days Later

"So, he's really an earl, then?" Cynthia asked suspiciously.

Prudy sighed. They'd been through this point several times on the seemingly endless carriage journey.

"Yes, Cynthia, he really is."

The two women were traveling together, for convenience and company more than anything else. Cythnia was going to Bainbridge, to meet her family, and Prudy was going to Rycroft Hall, to meet her husband.

Husband. What a strange idea that was.

After Prudy had made her shocking offer and had that offer accepted, things had moved quickly. Within a day, the few invites had gone out, with Prudy's name hastily replacing Catherine's. Another day, and the wedding took place.

It had been a quick, untidy affair, gone by in a flash. Prudy didn't even get a new gown for the occasion. Vows were said, rings exchanged, then Lord Rycroft was hobbling out of the church as fast as his bad leg would carry him, crawling into a carriage and setting off with a peremptory wave.

There was not, naturally, a wedding breakfast, or celebration of any kind.

"Feel free to join me at Rycroft Hall whenever you like, *wife*," Lord Rycroft had told her, leaning out of the carriage window. "I'm in no hurry, and I'm sure you aren't, either."

"Whenever I like?" Prudy had repeated, feeling awkward.

"Yes, and that includes *never*."

With these pleasant parting words, Lord Rycroft withdrew his head back into the carriage, and set off at once, leaving his uncle to soak up the few congratulations and collect the wedding gifts.

And that was that. The ceremony itself lasted no more than an hour, ending in Prudy as a real married woman, albeit without a husband. She'd trudged back home and began to pack at once. There was no point staying here – nobody was even talking to her. Catherine didn't seem to know what to say, and Prudy suspected that her sister felt almost guilty over the whole business. Jasper was clearly furious with his youngest daughter, mostly for stealing the match he'd planned for Catherine and throwing away her own potential with Isaac Bates – not that Prudy had ever wanted to marry him – and all but forcing him to agree to let Catherine marry whoever she liked.

Lydia never spoke much to anyone in any case.

And that brought Prudy to this point, travelling with her dubious closest friend, her luggage and things lashed to the roof of the carriage, driving along a rutted, heavily wooded forest road.

"It's just that Dalton Woods is such a ridiculous speck of land," Cynthia continued, twitching back the curtains to look out at the rain, "and no real earl would accept it. It's a silly little bit of land, with a silly little title given to him by his uncle."

"Well, considering that I am also the silly little wife given to him by his uncle, I'm not sure I can complain," Prudy pointed out sweetly, and Cynthia had the grace to blush.

"No offence meant," she muttered. Prudy didn't wholly believe her.

"I thought he was handsome, though," Prudy added, after a few moments of uncomfortable silence. "He's not what I expected."

"He wasn't hideous," Cynthia acknowledged ungraciously. "Although he looked like he was dressed for a funeral rather than for a wedding. All that black! The man dresses like someone three times his age."

"I thought he wore it well."

She sniffed. "You really must convince him to dress better, Prudy."

"And how am I meant to do that?"

"You're his wife, you little fool."

"That does not answer my question!"

Cynthia rolled her eyes. "I'm sure you'll manage. Oh, and do try and do something about those awful pockmarks on his face and neck. A little powder might cover them up."

Prudy shifted. "I hardly noticed them. I don't want to make him feel uncomfortable about them, in any case."

Her friend shot her a pitying look. "As you like, dear. You know, the stories about him being a monster are almost certainly false."

Prudy sighed. "Do you mean a monster that turns into a wolf at the full moon and stalks the forest, or the kind who drinks too much, beats his wife, and mistreats his servants? In my experience, the latter kind is more common."

Cynthia pursed her lips. "Well, I've heard stories of both. Not the wife-beating, of course, on account of Lord Rycroft never having been married before. But you aren't listening, dear. I said they were *probably* false."

"You know, if you intended to reassure me, you're doing a bad job of it."

Her friend bridled. "I was only trying to be helpful."

Prudy drew in a long, steadying breath. She thought, not for the first time, that taking this trip with Cynthia was a huge mistake.

She missed her sister. Catherine had hugged Prudy so tightly when she left, tears pricking in both of their eyes.

"Be safe, my darling girl," Catherine whispered. "Write to me. Say the word, and I'll come at once, and fetch you away."

"Oh, that won't be necessary," Prudy had said, with more confidence than she felt. "I'll be fine. I always intended to marry eventually, and now I've married an *earl*."

And he *was* an earl, regardless of Cynthia's barbed comments.

It was a relief when they reached Cynthia's country seat home, a wide, ugly mansion built on the edge of a vast forest, the trees stretching out further than the eye could see. This was Dalton woods, which Cynthia had insisted was inhabited by ghosts, monsters, and all sorts of vile creatures. Lord Rycroft not least of all, it seemed.

The carriage stopped, and a couple of footmen hurried out, heads ducked against the rain, to start unloading Cynthia's possessions. The woman in question hesitated, poised to clamber out of the carriage.

"You could stay with us for a while, if you like," she said, in a rush. "Mama and Papa would not object, I'm sure. Just to catch your breath, to rest for a day or two while the weather clears up."

Prudy bit her lip. "That's kind of you, Cynthia, truly it is. But... but I think I'd better face my fate sooner or later. I want to reach Rycroft Hall today."

Cynthia opened her mouth, as if intending to argue. She closed it again, and simply nodded.

"Well, as you like. I hope you'll come and see me as soon as you're settled. And... and good luck, Prudy."

Prudy smiled weakly. "Thank you."

Then Cynthia climbed out, shawl pulled over her head to shelter her from the rain and went running inside. Prudy observed the illuminated windows of Roland House, glowing like golden squares of warm butter, with Cynthia's mother gracefully positioned within, gazing indulgently at her daughter hastening up the path.

Something ached in Prudy's chest. She sat back, cutting off her view of the pleasant, welcoming house. She banged on the roof of the carriage.

"Drive on!" she ordered, and the vehicle lurched forward, heading straight for the woods. As they plunged into the leafy green darkness, Prudy closed her eyes.

Please let me be doing the right thing.

After all, it's far too late to change my mind.

***

They had been travelling for an hour, maybe two, when Prudy was jerked from an uneasy sleep by the scream of a horse, and the carriage lurching forward and sideways. She was thrown out of the seat into the one opposite. The carriage lurched again, and she found herself wedged on the floor between the two carriage seats, heart pounding.

They'd stopped.

There were a few shouts from the coachman, and then the door was wrenched open. Water dripped from the wide brim of his hat, and he blinked to see Prudy on the floor, stuffed between the carriage seats.

"Hole in the road, Miss," he said shortly. "We've lost a wheel."

"Oh. Oh, dear," Prudy muttered, struggling to her feet. "Let me take a look."

The coachman looked as though he'd rather she stayed in the carriage, but he reluctantly offered her a hand to clamber out

43

onto the muddy bank.

Sure enough, a tremendous hole in the road had caught the front wheel of the carriage, smashing the wheel itself and damaging the underside of the carriage. The vehicle lurched drunkenly to one side, as if it planned to tip itself into the bank and roll away into the forest. Prudy tried not to look at the forest itself. The road was long and straight, not particularly well cared for, and the thick woodland loomed on either side, the tree branches almost meeting above their heads. They were well into the afternoon now, and already the light was fading away.

The horses, she was pleased to notice, were quite safe, standing in their traces with a look of mild annoyance.

"We can't fix this," Prudy stated. The coachman barely held back a roll of his eyes.

"No, Miss, we can't. Only thing to do is to wait for a passer-by to help us."

Prudy bit her lip. "And have we seen any?"

"What?"

"Have we seen any passers-by? We've been travelling on this road for hours, and I don't believe we've passed another carriage or even a horse rider. We could be here all night."

The coachman did not seem pleased at this logic. "Somebody will come by," he repeated, as if she was slow in grasping the concept.

Prudy tugged on her coat, glad now that she'd brought a proper coat and hat instead of the light, pretty shawl her mother had recommended. Her boots, at the very least, were sturdy.

"How far to Rycroft Hall?" she said at last. "It's a straight road, is it not? Impossible to get lost, according to the map."

The coachman seemed displeased at the mention of *maps*. Perhaps he did not think ladies should bother their pretty heads with looking at maps.

"Eight miles," he said shortly. "Five to the nearest town."

"Five miles. I can manage five miles."

The man blinked. "What's that, Miss?"

"I'll walk to the town and send back help. It seems the most sensible thing to do."

The coachman looked aggrieved. "I can't allow that, Miss."

"You must," she said sweetly. "Wait here. I shan't be long."

44

"Then I must go with you."

"I'd prefer for you to wait with the luggage. I'd rather not arrive at my husband's home without a single trinket to my name. Sit inside the carriage, if you like. It'll be drier."

She turned and began to walk purposefully away, but the coachman called after her.

"Miss, I really can't allow..."

"It's not *miss* anymore," Prudy called back over her shoulder. "I'm Lady Rycroft now."

***

It had been, Prudy reflected, a mistake.

The rain only got heavier. Her straw bonnet was not equipped to deal with that sort of rain, and water dripped freely from the brim, soaking through to wet her head. Sopping curls mingled with the soaked ribbon sticking to her neck, and water trickled past the collar of her coat. The shoulders and elbows of her coat seemed particularly wet, and the hem of her skirt was at least twelve inches deep in mud and water.

At least my boots aren't leaking, Prudy thought miserably.

The road had seemed dead straight, but at some point she had looked behind and the carriage and coachman had vanished, like they'd never been there.

Keep going, she told herself grimly. *You made this happen. You saved Catherine. You... you saved yourself, really. Papa was probably going to make you marry someone awful.*

She trudged onwards, teeth gritted. Five miles had not seemed like a lot when she was back at the carriage, but now... now every step hurt. Her boots might not be leaking but they were starting to rub at her feet. She was getting a blister.

It was freezing too, no matter how fast Prudy walked, not that she had the energy to do much at the moment. Wrapping her arms around herself, Prudy put her head down into the growing wind, ice-cold rain driving into her face. Her bonnet was blown off her head, only saved from whipping away by the ribbon knotted around her neck. Prudy gritted her teeth and pushed onwards.

And then, almost without warning, the path opened up, and the trees pulled back, and she found herself staring at a neat little

45

town.

The town was an unusual one, the houses built high instead of wide, and the forest still seemed to hem them in closely. Lights burned in almost every window, and suddenly it seemed much less dark than before.

The sign at the entrance to the clearing read *Dalton Town*.

Teeth chattering, Prudy lurched along a cobbled road winding through the little town, looking for an inn.

She found one. The windows blazed with lights, and when the door creaked open to let a drunkard stagger out, she heard laughter and chatter come drifting out.

It was not, of course, appropriate for a woman to go staggering into a public house at this hour of the evening, soaked to the skin and *alone*, but Prudy did not have time or energy to think about propriety. She all but hurled herself against the door and went stumbling inside.

A delicious wall of warmth hit her, and Prudy staggered to a halt.

Silence immediately fell, and she felt the eyes of every person in the room on her.

All men, of course. Most of them looked like ordinary village men, enjoying a pint of ale after a hard day's work, foam still smeared over their wispy beards.

"My... my carriage hit a pothole," Prudy gasped, blinking water out of her eyes. She could have sworn that a few parts of her were literally freezing. "Could I have some assistance?"

For a long half-minute, there was no response. A pang of fear started to creep along Prudy's limbs, as for the first time she wondered what would happen if nobody offered to help.

Then a man stood up.

He was sitting with a group of reasonably well-dressed gentlemen, all circled around a table with a game of cards in progress.

"We shall help you," the man said, with the confident authority that came from somebody accustomed to being obeyed. "John, Marcus, fetch the horses. How far along is your carriage broken down, my lady?"

"Five miles back down the road," Prudy answered, almost sagging with relief. "The coachman stayed with the carriage. The

46

wheel is entirely broken."

"Not to worry, we've repaired similar things before. We'll have you on your way in no time. Where are you trying to get to?"

"Rycroft Hall."

There was a faint murmuring at this, and a few people exchanged significant looks. Prudy swallowed hard, brushing back wet curls from where they stuck to her forehead.

As she warmed up slowly, she began to realize just what a sight she must look. Her dress and coat were soaked, her bonnet hanging crazily down her back. She was covered in mud and rainwater, deathly pale, teeth chattering vigorously. Prudy had no doubt that her hair was flattened to her head, wet and lank, and her face was waxy and blotchy.

She was, to say the least, not looking her best.

The man who'd spoken first came around the table towards her. He was tall, broad-shouldered, sandy-haired, and handsome in a rollicking country sort of way. He was dressed well but not showily, and when he smiled kindly down at her, his smile was a pleasant one.

"My name is Patrick Devin," he said quietly. "You've had quite an ordeal, it seems. You were very brave to walk that far, in this weather."

"We didn't have much of a choice," she sniffled. "We hadn't seen a soul on our journey here, and I just knew that nobody would come to help us."

"You may well be right. Now, some of my friends and hired men will go at once to rescue your carriage and coachman. However, I am concerned that you might catch a cold. I propose to take you myself to Rycroft Hall at once. However, if you would prefer otherwise, then I must insist on you staying here for the night."

Prudy sighed. She was beginning to feel a bit more human, but some of the discomforts remained. Her wet clothes chafed her skin, and her boots hurt so much that both of her feet were throbbing and numb.

The inn was warm, at the very least, but it wouldn't make for a comfortable night's stay. And then, what would be the point of all this? She might as well have stayed at Cynthia's for another night.

47

I just want to get it over with.

"I'd like to go on to Rycroft Hall," Prudy said, as firmly as she could manage. "If you'll take me."

Patrick smiled. "Of course. Give me a moment to get my horse ready. I suppose you don't have any dry clothes to change into?"

"No, I don't, but they'd probably only get wet on the way."

He chuckled appreciatively and left her to bask in the warmth of the inn for a few more minutes.

Fifteen minutes later, a crowd of men set off from the inn. The majority of them headed down the main path, on the lookout for a damaged carriage and a miserable coachman, and one gentleman on horseback, with a lady behind him, took a narrower track which led deep into the woods.

Prudy did not particularly enjoy sitting up behind a man's saddle, but it was better than walking, and she felt a trifle better now that she'd been able to warm up properly. The rain still fell, but the path Patrick Devin led them down was so thickly framed by trees and foliage that very little rain made its way down to them. The cold was still biting, and the dark was absolute, but the horse was sure-footed and the path even enough.

They trotted along in silence for a few moments, while Prudy tried not to think of the awkwardness of riding on the back of a horse with a man she had only just met.

None of this would have happened if my wretch of a husband would just have let me come back with him, she thought sourly.

And then, quite abruptly, they were there.

Prudy had expected a long, winding drive, raked gravel perhaps, with a strip of neatly manicured greenery on either side. Instead, they continued along the path they were on, just about wide enough for a carriage, and then turned a corner and were faced with tall, wrought-iron gates.

A sign was tied to the gates: *Private, No Trespassing.*

"Lovely," she commented, eyeing the rusted chains hanging from the iron bars. The chains were at least left unlocked. She was expected, then.

Patrick was moving to slide down from his horse, no doubt to open the gates and go inside, but Prudy grabbed his shoulder.

48

"I'll go on alone from here. The house is just there."

He frowned. "I'd much rather escort you myself."

"You've been remarkably kind, sir, and I hope soon to be able to thank you properly, but I believe it would be bad form to arrive at one's husband's home for the first time on horseback with another man. We aren't expecting guests, you see."

Patrick flinched, staring. "Husband…? Do you mean to say that you are married? To Lord Rycroft?"

She swallowed. "Yes, that's correct. It's a very recent thing."

The man let out a long breath. "Well, I never. I knew he'd gone into town, but marriage… *Gideon*? Goodness. This has been a shocking night, and no mistake. Oh, eh, my congratulations, of course."

"Thank you," Prudy managed, sliding off the back of the horse. She landed in a puddle with a *splosh*. Wonderful. "And I do mean it. You've been so kind, I really can't…"

"Please, Miss… eh, I suppose it would Lady Rycroft, actually. Please, Lady Rycroft, get yourself inside and out of this weather. I hope to see you again soon."

He touched the brim of his hat, and Prudy gave up, shoving open the rusted gates and hurrying up the cobbled drive towards her new home.

When she turned around, Patrick Devin was gone.

The house loomed in front of her, and Prudy tried not to look too hard at it. Lights glimmered in a few windows, but mostly the vast, sprawling building was dark and silent. Ivy clustered around the bone-white stone, and the dark windows seemed to be watching her approach. The garden on either side was overgrown and tangled, more of a jungle than the forest she'd just left behind. Weeds and grass sprouted thickly between the cobbles, and plenty of them were missing, nearly causing her to twist an ankle more than once.

The whole place was like something out of Mrs Radcliffe's wild imagination.

I want to go home, Prudy thought, as fiercely as a child, and she felt like crying.

She'd nearly reached the wide, well-worn stone steps that led up to the front door when the door itself opened.

A woman in her fifties stood there, with a well-lined face, a plump body, and iron-grey hair scraped back into a bun. She held a lantern, and Prudy scrambled gratefully towards the warm light.

"You must be the new Lady Rycroft," the woman said shortly. "I'm the housekeeper. My name is Agatha Moss. You're later than we expected."

"I'm sorry," Prudy said, wondering why she was apologizing to her own housekeeper about something entirely beyond her control.

Agatha grunted. "Well, you're here now. Come in."

Without waiting for a reply, Agatha turned and marched back along the hallway, taking the light with her. There was little else to do but follow her, so Prudy did just that.

Chapter Six

Prudy had hoped to get a really good look at her new home, but she was destined to be disappointed.

The cavernous hall behind the door was almost completely dark, with only a few shafts of weak, silvery moonlight streaming in through the windows to illuminate cold marble floors and a few massive, austere portraits hanging on the walls. Aside from that, she only got the impression of a vast space, no doubt with countless doors opening off it. The buttery glow of Agatha's lantern bobbed along, the single light in the darkness, and Prudy was obliged to scuttle after it.

The place was quiet, too, and her wet boots made unseemly squelching noises on the marble floor.

"It's very dark in here," Prudy gasped out at last. "I thought there'd be... candles, or something like that. Or a fire."

Agatha twisted to look back at her. "Candles? A fire? What, here in the Great Hall? What a terrible waste. Nobody uses these rooms after dark. The master goes to his study, and the rest of us sit in the kitchen until it's time for bed. No sense wasting candles on empty rooms, is there?"

She swallowed. "It would be cosier."

Agatha shot her a look.

"*Cosy*, eh? Well, you'll be the mistress from now on, so if you want to waste a fortune on countless good wax candles, burning with nobody to see or appreciate them, I suppose you may do it."

Prudy sighed. "I didn't say that."

She was vaguely aware that Agatha was showing what Lydia Copperwell would call *impertinence*. She'd had a real horror of the servants back at the Copperwell home becoming *impertinent*, which to Prudy's recollection seemed to involve not being subservient enough or explaining that something was not actually their fault.

"We thought you weren't coming tonight," Agatha added over her shoulder. "What with the rain and it getting so dark. If one of the boys from the inn hadn't run ahead to let us know you were on your way, the gates would have been locked. Still, there'll be a bath ready soon, and your room is all prepared."

51

The idea of a bath almost made Prudy weak at the knees. However, there was another concern she hadn't thought about.

"My room?" she repeated cautiously. "Is Lord Rycroft..."

"Lord Rycroft's room is in the other wing," Agatha answered steadfastly, not looking around. "You'll be in the Green Room, which was always Lady Rycroft's room in years gone by."

Prudy relaxed a little. She wouldn't have to share a room with her husband, then, thank heavens. That was something.

"I wouldn't say no to a bath," she said, unable to keep the relief from her voice. "I'm soaking and freezing."

Agatha twisted to look back at her. "Where's the carriage, my lady? And your things?"

"Ah. Well, that is actually a strange story..."

They finally reached the end of the massive Great Hall, reaching a wide, twisting set of stairs, carpeted with an old red runner down the middle. Their footsteps echoed as Prudy talked, explaining the accident with the carriage, and the help of the locals. She found herself glossing over her own walk, but Agatha paused at the top of the stairs, shooting a beady stare at Prudy.

"You walked five miles in the pouring rain? Alone, at this time of night?"

Prudy wasn't sure what to respond, but apparently no response was needed. Agatha gave a low whistle, then turned, leading the way along a dark hallway.

As far as Prudy could tell, there was a large, circular landing at the top of the stairs, with hallways shooting off like spokes of a wheel. She would have liked to explore a little, perhaps, since her delightful husband was probably in bed already, but Agatha was striding away down one hallway and Prudy was obliged to follow.

"Do you know a man named Patrick Devin?" Prudy called, hurrying to catch up with the servant. "He brought me here. Seemed to know the way pretty well, actually. He was very kind."

Agatha sighed. "He and the master were close friends, years ago. That was before... ahem. Folks grow apart, I suppose. It's a pity, but Master Patrick was always a fine young man. I'm not surprised he went the extra mile to bring you here."

"Perhaps we could invite him here for tea," Prudy suggested. "He and Lord Rycroft might reconnect."

Agatha made a gasping, coughing sound that might have

been a smothered laugh, and cast a pitying glance over her shoulder.

"Perhaps we will, your ladyship, perhaps we will. Ah, this is your room."

And just like that, their long, dark walk through Prudy's new home was over. An open door appeared around a twist in the hallway, a rectangle of warm light, and Prudy stepped gratefully inside.

Her new room was at least three times as large as her room back home. There was a blazing fire, filling the room with warmth, and a sofa and low coffee table set in front of it. The bed was huge, a four poster, set up on a platform and piled so high with blankets and feather pillows that if Prudy hadn't been so wet and shivery, she might have gone and thrown herself into it. There were wardrobes and trunks, of course, and Prudy felt a pang of regret that she couldn't put any of her clothes into them yet. Another door opened into another, smaller room – a private washroom.

Prudy had never experienced such luxury.

"There's not much green in here," was all she could manage.

Agatha chuckled. "Yes, indeed. There used to be, but the master got an odd fancy about the wallpaper, and had it all taken down."

A pair of young women, maids, were staggering in and out of the washroom with buckets, steam billowing out around them. The girls seemed to be sisters, with the same lank blonde hair and large, doll-blue eyes, and they gasped at the sight of Prudy.

Well, she was sure that she *did* present quite an unusual sight.

"Did you get caught in the rain, miss?" the younger-looking girl asked, eyes wide. The older one elbowed her.

"It's Lady Rycroft, Daisy," she hissed. The girl blushed.

"It's quite alright, Daisy," Prudy managed, feeling that she ought to say *something*. I ran into quite a lot of bad luck on my way here. But I'm here now, and Mrs Moss tells me you've run me a lovely, hot bath."

Daisy perked up. "That we have, miss... I mean, Lady Rycroft. We set out a nightgown for you, too, and a robe and some slippers, just in case you didn't get yours unpacked in time."

The older girl elbowed her again. "*We'll* be the ones

53

unpacking, Daisy, you fool."

"My things haven't arrived," Prudy added quickly. "It's a long story. But thank you, girls, for the bath. It's exactly what I would have wanted after such a long day."

Prudy glanced at Agatha, just in time to see the older woman flash her an approving smile.

"Rose, Daisy, is the bath prepared?"

"That was the last bucket," the older girl said. "We'll help Lady Rycroft wash, won't we? Only I've never waited on a fine lady before, and so..."

"That won't be necessary, thank you," Prudy said hurriedly. "I'm quite used to bathing myself, you see, and there's no point changing now. Besides, it's late, and I'm sure you were all in the middle of resting for tomorrow. I'll be fine, thank you."

The girls shot a glance at Agatha, who answered with a slow, stately nod. Rose and Daisy bobbed lopsided curtsies and scurried out, whispering eagerly to each other as soon as they were out of the door.

Is this all the servants they have? Prudy thought, with a flash of worry. *In this big old house?*

She hadn't had the chance to look around, but everything had seemed rather *dusty*. Big houses like this got dirty very quickly. Agatha probably had little time for cleaning, and if the housework all fell on the shoulders of those two...

Prudy sighed, unbuttoning her coat. The feeling had come back to her fingers, at the very least. A quick peek in the washroom revealed a large copper tub, full of deliciously warm water, with bathing sheets and a nightgown hanging nearby. Prudy could almost feel the hot water on her skin.

"Are you sure about bathing alone, Lady Rycroft?" Agatha asked, helping Prudy unlace the back of her gown. "You've had a long day."

"I'll start as I mean to go on, Mrs Moss. And I'm sure there'll be plenty to do without my being dressed and washed like a doll. You've done quite enough, thank you."

Agatha allowed herself a small smile. "Well, that's good news, and no mistake. I'll launder your wet things, and your trunks should have arrived by morning. There's a bell pull in the corner of the room, if you need anything. And do call me Agatha, Lady

Rycroft. *Mrs Moss* was my mother."

Prudy had to smile at that. Exhaustion was starting to creep in, now that she had reached her destination at last. Part of her wondered what Lord Rycroft was doing. Did he know she was here?

Do I want him to know I'm here?

Inside the washroom, Prudy took off the rest of her clothes – also damp – and handed them out to Agatha.

"Sleep well, Lady Rycroft. It's good that you're here, at last."

Prudy paused before the door, frowning. Was it her imagination, or was there something odd in Agatha's voice? Before she could ask, footsteps retreated, and the door closed softly. Agatha had gone, then.

The lure of the bath was too much, then, and Prudy hurried over to it, bare feet slapping on the floor. Sliding into the water was the most delicious thing she'd ever experienced in her life. It was a deep bath, and Prudy could submerge herself up to her nose, if she wished. She tilted her head back, closing her eyes.

Maybe it won't be so bad here. If he stays in his study all the time and leaves me alone, then...

There was a rap on the door, no doubt Agatha forgetting something.

"Come in," Prudy called, drowsy already.

The door opened, and Lord Gideon Rycroft stood there.

He jerked back at the sight of Prudy in the bathtub, and she squealed, diving deeper into the bath, water churning and slopping over the sides.

"What are you doing here?" she gasped.

"I knocked, and you said to come in!"

"I thought you were Agatha!"

"Well, I'm not! I beg your pardon, I'll..." he turned to go, but Prudy sighed impatiently.

"Oh, just say what you wanted to say. You can't see anything from there, anyway."

He cleared his throat, turning back. In the flickering golden light spilling from the bedroom, Lord Rycroft looked like a great, pale shadow, filling the doorway. His expression was hard to read, and Prudy began to wish she'd waited until the warm, safe light of day to come here.

"I came to ask you what you thought you were doing," he said shortly.

"I don't understand."

"Why are you here, Prudence?"

She frowned. "It's Prudy. And I'm your wife – or did you forget already?"

"That doesn't answer my question. Why are you *here*?"

"To be your wife, of course."

He narrowed his eyes. "And what do you think a wife does?"

She shrugged, flicking water across the surface of the tub. "Hosting, I suppose. Managing the household tasks, overseeing the food preparation. Companionship, you know."

Lord Rycroft – she ought to think of him as *Gideon* now, since they were, after all, married – shifted his weight off his bad leg.

"I've never been one for much companionship," he said brusquely. "Agatha manages the household tasks and food, and I'm no host. To be frank, Prudence, there's really nothing for you to do here. You're quite unnecessary. There's no place for you, I'm afraid."

Harsh words to hear from one's new husband. Prudy watched the glitter of candles reflect in the surface of the bath.

"Well, there was no place for me at home, either," she said shortly. "I was unnecessary there, too. I was supposed to be a boy, you know. I managed then, dear husband, and I'll manage here too."

Gideon blinked, as if she'd taken him by surprise.

"I see," he answered after a pause. "Thank you for making that clear. Sleep well."

Was it her imagination, or did that *sleep well* sound more like a warning than well-wishing? There was no time to ask for clarification, because Gideon left immediately, closing both the door of the washroom and the door to Prudy's room behind him.

She sank further down into the bath, letting the hot water seep into her body, soothing aching muscles and warming frozen fingers and toes.

He's the oddest man I have ever met, Prudy thought, a little nervously. *He doesn't want me here, but I can't possibly go home now.*

56

Besides, now I want to prove that wretch wrong. There'll be a place for me here, and I'm determined to find it.

***

Despite Prudy's exhaustion, sleep did not come easily. A heavy grandfather clock in the corner ticked off the minutes, keeping her awake. The clock face claimed that it was close to one o' clock in the morning, and Prudy could believe it.

Back home, there were always lights somewhere. A couple of candles in a hallway, streetlamps outside, the warm squares of lit windows in the distance. She'd gone to the window earlier and pulled back the heavy velvet curtains. The rain was heavier than ever, clouds covering up even the moon and stars. All she could see was black.

It was horribly oppressive.

The fire had long since died down, and the water in the bathtub was ice cold, since Prudy hadn't been able to bring herself to ring the bell and get the maids to empty it. In a fit of frugality, she'd gone around blowing out all of the candles but one, assuming that she would long be asleep by the time the fire died down. She regretted that now, but there was no tinderbox to be found.

The single candle flickered on Prudy's bedside table, and she watched it from within her nest of blankets and pillows.

The bed was comfortable, at least.

Surely, I'll fall asleep eventually, she thought despairingly.

And then came the footsteps.

At first, Prudy told herself it was just the creak and groan of an old house settling at night, but the noise came gradually closer and closer until it was impossible to pretend that it was anything except *footsteps*.

Prudy sat slowly upright, eyes fixed on the door. There was a key in the lock, but she hadn't turned it. Why hadn't she turned it?

She strained her eyes, trying to make out any irregularity in the footsteps that might indicate they came from Gideon and his bad leg, but it was impossible to tell. The footsteps drew closer and closer, and Prudy sat stock still, eyes burning, hands fisted in the blankets.

57

The footsteps seemed to halt by her door. She held her breath, waiting for the doorknob to turn.

Then they continued, passing by her door and fading away. Prudy let out a long, ragged breath. Forcing herself out of bed, she hurried across the room, terrified that a creaking floorboard would bring the owner of the footsteps back. Surely whoever it was would have seen the weak light coming from underneath her door?

She turned the key in the lock, and dived back to bed as if blankets might save her from an intruder.

It's probably just a servant, she told herself, *doing a late-night patrol to make sure that everything is well. I'm going to feel silly in the morning.*

She didn't feel silly now, though. Suddenly, Prudy's room seemed full of jumping shadows, and the dying firelight and candle weren't enough, not nearly enough. Wouldn't an old house like this have endless secret passages, and ways for a servant to enter the room secretly? How would she know?

Fear clawed its way up Prudy's throat like bile, and she burrowed deep in the blankets, eyes still fixed on the door.

Although, danger might come crawling through the wardrobe, or from a secret panel in the washroom...

Stop it! This isn't a Gothic novel, you fool! It's just a creaky old house and a wakeful servant, that's all!

Unfortunately, her fears were not to be reasoned away. Prudy lay awake for hours, only finally falling asleep when the pink and gold of dawn finally touched the horizon.

Chapter Seven

She wasn't dead in the morning, which was an excellent start.

Prudy lay there for a few moments, waking up, and tried to come to terms with her new reality.

This is it, then. This is the first day of the rest of my life.

In broad daylight, Prudy felt stupid for imagining monsters in the shadows. The footsteps outside her door were almost certainly a servant patrolling at night, but they might well have been a vivid dream. After all, she'd had a chaotic day.

There was a tap on the door, making her flinch.

"Who is it?"

"It's Agatha, Lady Rycroft. I came earlier to bring your breakfast, but the door was locked. I thought it best to let you sleep, although I'll be frank – I was getting a little worried."

Prudy bounced out of bed – the remarkable bed *had* been shockingly comfortable – and hurried across to unlock the door.

Agatha was standing there, a breakfast tray in her hands, and looked extremely relieved.

"I started to worry you might have dozed off in your bath," she said, a trifle reproving. "Folks can drown that way."

"Well, I've gone many years in life without drowning in the bathtub, so I hope I might manage a few more yet," Prudy said, venturing a small smile.

Agatha shook her head, but there was a fondness to it now. She brought the breakfast tray into the room, setting it down on the bed.

"Once you've breakfasted, my lady, I'll start bringing up your clothes and things, and the girls will put them away. They arrived early this morning, so you can start to properly settle in. I suppose you'd like a tour, afterwards?"

Prudy hesitated, imagining Agatha striding through the house like she had before, barely stopping for breath.

"I think I'll go for a wander myself, Agatha, if that's all the same for you. I think I ought to explore my new home alone."

Agatha did not seem to approve.

"As you like, Lady Rycroft, as you like." She turned to go, but

Prudy spoke up again.

"It's an odd question, Agatha, but do any of the servants walk around the house at night? To be sure that all the candles are out, all the windows and doors locked, and so on? A footman, perhaps?"

Agatha turned back, frowning. "We don't have much in the way of footmen here, Lady Rycroft. The girls wouldn't stir from their rooms after dark, not if they could help it. You know how silly young girls get about old houses like this. There are a hundred haunting stories, at the very least. I can't think of who'd be walking around at night."

A chill rolled down Prudy's spine, and goosebumps prickled over her skin.

"I... I see. What about Lord Rycroft?"

"No," Agatha said firmly. "Not him."

Prudy wasn't sure she believed her, but pressing the subject further might make her seem a little unhinged. Besides, there was no proof that the footsteps were anything more than a dream.

"I see," she said faintly. "Thank you, Agatha. That will be all."

***

Prudy had expected rooms full of dust, heavy with cobwebs. She'd expected to be greeted by a musty, stale smell in each room, the smell of a place never aired out and even less frequently cleaned.

She was pleasantly surprised.

While there were plenty of rooms covered up with dust covers and shut up – the huge, silent ballroom, for one – the rooms that were open were immaculate. Oh, she could find a fingertip of dust here and there, and the occasional cobweb hanging too high for the average maid with a duster to reach, but there was no denying that the rooms were clean, well-aired, and pleasant.

The Great Hall, which she'd crossed the previous night, was impeccably clean, her muddy footsteps already mopped away, the floor gleaming. The portraits were nonetheless unsettling, though. Prudy identified Gideon's uncle, the Marquess of Derby, looking a little less portly in his portrait. There was another of Gideon, younger, without the faint pockmarks on his neck and face.

60

She crossed the Great Hall to a wide hallway, in the opposite direction to the staircase. Prudy had already explored most of upstairs. It was mostly bedrooms, guest rooms, linen closets, and so on. There was a set of stairs leading to the attics, where the servants slept, and one wing was Gideon's, so she avoided that, too.

Downstairs was even more sprawling. No neat hallways with doors branching off it, each one leading to another unused guest room – there were morning rooms, empty studies, a library of course, and room after room full of white-swathed furniture and silence. A few rooms were locked, but a quick peek through the keyhole was always disappointing – more shrouded furniture and not much else.

It was much, much bigger to the home Prudy was used to. A person could get lost in here, but the rooms were set out in a surprisingly orderly and logical fashion. She'd already curved back on herself twice, finding herself in the middle of the Great Hall again.

However, there wasn't a great deal of light coming into the rooms, sparkling windows notwithstanding. The velvet curtains were dark and heavy, and diligently kept out most of the day's sunlight. Coupled with the dark wood and old-fashioned furniture of the place, Rycroft Hall could not by any stretch of the imagination be described as *light and airy,* which was of course all the rage in modern houses these days.

She would have to see what she could do about that.

Footsteps echoed behind her, and Prudy just had time to jump before Agatha came puffing in, red-faced.

"There you are, Lady Rycroft. I've been combing the house for you."

"I'm sorry," Prudy said, not bothering to wonder why she was apologising so much to her housekeeper. "Is luncheon ready?"

"Nearly, your ladyship. It'll be on in the dining room – can you find it?"

"I should think so. Will Lord Rycroft be joining?"

Agatha blinked. "I... I don't think so."

Prudy bit her lip. Of course, he was going to avoid her as best he could. She'd better get used to eating alone.

"I see. Was there anything else?"

"Actually, yes," Agatha whipped out a neat little envelope from her apron pocket, handing it over with a smile. "Your first correspondence here, your ladyship! The letter must have followed you down."

Prudy recognized her sister's handwriting at ten paces and had to fight not to snatch it away.

"That's wonderful, thank you, Agatha."

Agatha gave a nod. "I'll come back and inform you of luncheon time – we don't use a gong here. No point, when it's just Lord Rycroft sitting down to table. And you now, too, your ladyship."

"Of course. Thank you."

Agatha melted away, and Prudy dived into the nearest room. It was a morning-room, she thought, or a neat little parlour. Either way, it was immaculate, but clearly seldom used. Settling herself on a window seat, Prudy tore open the envelope.

It wasn't a long letter.

My dearest, darling Prudy,

I've been thinking of you nonstop. Mama and Papa don't talk about it all much — I know they planned for me to marry Lord Rycroft, and you to make another glorious match, but I suspect that Papa is just relieved not to have let his golden goose slip away at all.

By golden goose, I mean Lord Rycroft, naturally.

I have met with Simon again. I must gather my courage first, but you, my darling love, have given me a chance. You made Papa promise to let me marry who I liked. He doesn't imagine I'll introduce him to a tailor's apprentice, and I daresay he'll be furious, but I don't care. I'm going to introduce him to Simon and announce our betrothal right after. I must confess, I'm terrified.

I'm afraid for you, too, Prudy. Is Lord Rycroft as macabre and Gothic as we first thought? Is he kind to you? Please write as soon as you can and put me out of my misery. I hope that you can find happiness, my darling sister. If not, I shall come and take you away myself — that I can promise!

All my love,
Your sister,
Catherine

A short letter indeed, but Prudy didn't care. She pressed it to her chest, closing her eyes. Suddenly, the house seemed horribly quiet and still, and she was more alone than she could ever have imagined.

I wish Catherine was here. I wish… I wish Cynthia *were here.*

Prudy screwed up her face, closing her eyes tight and praying that she wouldn't cry. Not here, not in the life she'd *chosen*. Nobody had made her offer to marry Lord Rycroft. In this position, she'd outrank most of her friends, to say nothing of her own sister. She was a *married woman*, and that counted for something, even if her husband was busily pretending he didn't have a wife at all.

Footsteps echoed – that seemed to be a theme in Rycroft Hall – and Agatha poked her head in the door.

"Luncheon will be another half an hour. What about that letter? Good news?"

Prudy smiled wanly, realizing that she must look stricken.

"Oh, yes, my sister. She misses me, of course."

"Ahh," Agatha narrowed her gaze. "Miss Catherine Copperwell."

"You know her?"

"I know she was meant to be marrying the master. Do you think she would have been unhappy here, then?"

"I…" Prudy hesitated, trying to think of something to say. She was aware that this wasn't a normal conversation for a lady and her housekeeper to have. Agatha shifted, looking a little awkward.

"I don't mean to overstep, of course, Lady Rycroft. I don't mean to imply that you're not welcome, either. Some companionship for the master is long overdue, in my opinion."

"There was somebody else," Prudy said at last. She was aware that her mother would condemn this conversation as *pure impertinence*, but somehow it seemed that Agatha had a right to know. Besides, she'd been kind to Prudy. "For Catherine, I mean. Lord Rycroft would have been kind to her, I know. He offered her use of his stables, which was pleasant of him. Only, Catherine doesn't much like riding, not like I do. It was well that it all worked out the way it did. I'm not in love with anyone else, you see."

Agatha nodded. "Love can be a tricky business for a young person."

Prudy cleared her throat, tucking away the letter. She'd read it again later, and then write a letter in reply. Could she invite Catherine already? No, Catherine would want to stay and sort things out with Simon. For now, Prudy was on her own.

"I'd like to see the stables, actually," Prudy heard herself say. "Do I have time before luncheon?"

Agatha hesitated. "Well, yes, but... well, I think you'll be a little disappointed, Lady Rycroft."

Lady Rycroft. That title still sounded so strange in Prudy's ears. She kept expecting some tall, thin, elegant woman in black silk and pearls to come sweeping out from somewhere, looking haughtily down her nose at everyone. That was the sort of person who should be called *Lady Rycroft*. Not *Prudy*.

"I'll be the judge of that," Prudy said, getting to her feet and shaking out her skirts. It was a pink muslin dress, pretty and simple, and it felt out of place here in this grand, dark old place. "Let's go, then."

"Oh," Prudy said, hands on her hips, looking around.

"Yes, that's what I was trying to tell you," Agatha said with a sigh. "Finest stables in this part of England, and what does he do? Uses them to keep a single horse."

The stables at Rycroft Hall were huge, easily big enough for twenty or thirty horses. More, maybe. And yet, all the stalls were empty. The stable was clean and tidy — which in Prudy's experience, a stable should never be *too* clean and tidy — and only one stall was occupied.

A bale of hay sat nearby, and a gleaming bridle and saddle hung from a hook above it. The leather was smooth and supple, the air heavy with the scent of freshly used polish and oil, and the brass of the buckles glowed like the sun.

The horse itself, a stallion, was huge, almost as big as the carthorses back home. This creature was stocky, but it was certainly no carthorse. It was larger by far than any of the ponies and horses Prudy had been permitted to ride, and she couldn't even imagine trying to put a side-saddle on that thing.

The horse was a dark grey colour, dappled on its back and flanks, with a long, thick black mane. Its coat was glossy, eyes gleaming with health, and there were no knots at all in its mane.

This was a horse better cared-for than any Prudy had ever seen.

The horse's name was on a brass plaque, placed on the front of the stall.

"*Cicero*," Prudy read aloud. "Curious name for a horse."

Agatha snorted. "What should the master have called it? Trotter? Silver? Cicero's a fine name."

"So, it's Lord Rycroft's horse, then? The groom must spend all of his time on this horse."

Agatha sighed. "No groom here. Lord Rycroft takes care of Cicero here himself. That horse got him through many a battle, he said, and he treats the creature like a child. Myself, I don't hold with horses. I'm no rider, and that one in particular would throw me as soon as it gave a look at me."

Prudy bit her lip, eyeing the horse. It was a fabulous creature, but not purebred. Perhaps that was why it was so strong and healthy. The horse tilted his head, eyeing her through liquid brown eyes. If she didn't know better, she might have said that it was suspicious.

"And there aren't any other horses?" she asked again. "What about for Lord Rycroft's carriage?"

"He generally borrows a pair of horses from the nearby farms. Cicero here wouldn't tolerate going into traces."

"Hm. Well, I did hope to ride sometime today. I could do with the fresh air, and I could explore a little. Do you think Lord Rycroft would mind if I borrowed Cicero?"

Agatha drew in a whistling breath through her teeth. "He surely would, Lady Rycroft. Even if he wouldn't, I couldn't in good conscience let you anywhere near that monster of a horse. He doesn't let *anyone* ride him besides the master."

Prudy bit her lip, eyeing the horse. Cicero stared boldly right back, as if daring her to come closer.

"I'm good with horses," she said, and took a step forward before Agatha could say a word.

Cicero snorted, jerking his head. She stretched out a hand, gingerly. With horses, Prudy had noticed that people were often too bold or too timid when they approached them. Like most things in life, balance was needed.

"What a beautiful creature you are," she murmured, hand still inches away from the horse's nose. He lifted his lip, as if not sure whether to snap or not. "Is he a war-horse, Agatha?"

"I believe so," Agatha managed, eyeing the horse with visible mistrust.

Prudy edged closer, gingerly placing her palm against the horse's warm, soft nose, ready to yank her hand away should a set of teeth come clacking.

Cicero met her gaze squarely for one heartbeat, then two, then the horse huffed and slid his head away, turning to nibble at the hay in his feeding box. Prudy took a step back, letting out a breath she hadn't realized she was holding.

"Well, I'll be," Agatha murmured. "Never seen that horse let anyone touch him. Nicely done, Lady Rycroft."

"Well, I'll have to earn Cicero's trust if I want to go riding, won't I?"

"I'm sure the master will buy you your own horse. Or you can get your own, once your allowance is all worked out."

Allowance. Of course. Prudy sucked in a breath. She would have money every quarter, as married ladies did. She was rich now.

An odd feeling, to say the very least.

I could buy my own horse. I'm a married woman, so I can choose what I want to buy. I could get a proper saddle and never ride side-saddle again. Gideon doesn't care what I do, does he? I'm free. I'm free.

The idea made her smile giddily.

Then a gong rang, echoing across the courtyard, making them both flinch.

"I asked Daisy to dig out the old gong and ring it when luncheon was ready," Agatha murmured. "I see she's found it. Are you ready to sit down to luncheon, Lady Rycroft?"

Prudy had hardly touched her breakfast, she'd been so excited about inspecting her new home, and now her stomach was gurgling, demanding food.

"More than ready, Agatha, thank you."

Agatha gave an approving nod. "And when you're ready with a letter to your sister, let me know, and I'll get it sent off as soon as possible."

Prudy smiled gratefully at the older woman.

At least I have one friend here, even if that friend isn't my husband. I'll find a place here. I will.

67

Chapter Eight

Gideon twitched back the curtain in his study, and watched his new wife stride out across the courtyard. There was a spring in her step, and she walked purposefully towards the stables.

He had no idea what she could be doing in there. There weren't any *horses*, for heaven's sakes.

Four days. Prudence had been here for four whole days, and Gideon had managed to avoid her almost constantly. It was an impressive feat, even in a house as big as theirs.

It wouldn't take much longer for her to get the hint, surely. She'd get bored, pack up, and go back to her family. She might even choose to go to London, enjoy some Society there. She could do that, now that she was married, and not worry about chaperones or gossip. He wondered if that idea had occurred to her yet.

It would, he was sure.

There was a tap on the door, making him jump, and Gideon just about managed to get back to his desk before the door opened.

"You should wait for me to tell you to come in, Agatha," Gideon pointed out peevishly.

Agatha sniffed, saying nothing. She was carrying a tea tray, having utilized that sixth sense of hers which just *knew* when Gideon was starting to feel peckish.

"You've been busy of late," she said, laying out the tea things and a plate of cakes. "Too busy even to poke your nose out of this study. One might expect a new-married man to take a little time off."

Gideon sighed. *This again.*

"The new Lady Rycroft is not staying, Agatha. There's nothing for her here."

"Nothing for her but her husband," Agatha pointed out. "Even if the man is trying to pretend she doesn't exist. She seems happy enough. What will you do if she stays?"

"She won't. Marriages like this aren't unheard of, you know. Two people marry for money or convenience, or any number of reasons, then they go their separate ways and live separate lives.

It's entirely normal."

"There's a difference between *not unheard of* and *normal.* Most married folks at least try to live a semblance of life together."

"I," Gideon said deliberately, "am not *normal.* I'm a monster, don't you know?"

She straightened up, crossing brawny arms across her chest. "I won't stand here and listen to your call yourself that."

"You could stand in the kitchen, then," Gideon suggested, lifting the lid of the teapot.

Of course, this was Agatha, who was not easily put off. She leaned forward, planting her hands on the desk, either side of the tea tray.

"Can I at least set a place for you at the dinner table tonight?"

"No," Gideon said firmly. "I'll take my dinner up here."

Agatha pressed her lips together. She looked... well, *disappointed.* Gideon ignored that thought. Agatha didn't understand. She thought that the world ought to see Gideon the way she did and was constantly surprised when it did not. If Agatha had her way, he'd saddle up Cicero and go trotting through the centre of town on market day, nodding proudly to everybody as he passed.

"That poor girl has eaten alone every meal since she arrived," Agatha said shortly. "It pains me to wait on her. If I wasn't the housekeeper, I'd pull out a chair for myself and at least keep her company."

"You can do that if you want. I won't stop you. I don't think she'd be happy, though."

Agatha scoffed, straightening up. "You don't know a thing about that girl, do you? She's no snob. She's been as pleasant as you please to all of us since she first arrived. She even helped Rose and Daisy polish the floors yesterday." She paused, blinking. "Not that they did much polishing. I think they were standing on cloths and racing each other... but that's neither here nor there. My point is, I think you'd be pleasantly surprised with her, Lord Rycroft."

Gideon flinched, like he always did when Agatha used his title. Wasn't there a time when he was just *Gideon* to her? Or even a pale, anxious little boy, loping after Joseph Smith, heading towards the stables. What was it they'd called him? A silly nickname, reluctantly dropped as he inched towards adulthood.

Giddy, that was it. *Come on, Giddy, I've got a new foal for you to see! The mare foaled just last night, and it's beautiful!*

Gideon swallowed hard, closing his eyes. It was a mistake to think about what was. It was always a mistake, a painful, hideous mistake.

"Why are you so keen for me to share my dinner table with that woman?" Gideon heard himself say.

Agatha's face tightened. "Because she's your wife. Because she's *lonely*, that's why. This big old place, nobody coming to call, no one but a handful of servants to spend time with. It's not right, Gideon, and you know it."

He flinched at his name. Nothing sounded right anymore – not *Lord Rycroft*, not *Gideon*.

"She doesn't have to stay," he heard himself say, defensive. Like a child. "She's welcome to leave whenever she wants. I'm not going to keep her here. I'm not going to get in the way of her living the life she wants. I just want to be left alone. I didn't *want* a wife. If she wants company, she should seek out my uncle – he's the one who wanted me to marry."

He's the one who blackmailed me into it, Gideon thought, but carefully didn't say it. He could imagine the flinch, the look of hurt on Agatha's face when she realized that, in a way, she was responsible.

No, that he *held* her responsible. Those were two different accusations, really. Guilt colouring his face, Gideon looked away.

There was a pie out on the tray, filling the air with a delicious, savoury scent, but his appetite had fled.

"It's better if she goes, Agatha," he murmured. "You know that."

"No, I don't know that. I don't know anything of the sort. Do you know what your problem is, Gideon?"

He sighed, leaning back in his chair. "I'm sure you're going to tell me."

Very few – if any – lords would submit to being told *what their problem was* by a housekeeper, no less, but Gideon had never minded Agatha's forthrightness. It was refreshing. Or something. Even if the whole world lied to his face, Agatha would tell him the truth. She didn't see him as clearly as they did, of course, but that wasn't her fault. She'd tell him the truth as she believed it. If she liked Prudence, then that was a mark in the young woman's favour.

"You're stubborn," Agatha said shortly.

Gideon sighed. "I thought you were going to tell me something new, Agatha."

"I mean it. You make up your mind about something, you dig in your heels, and you won't change your opinion, not for anything. There's a difference between pig-headedness and strength of mind, you know."

"I know, Agatha, I know. Do you really think, though, that my dear wife's joy and comfort will be improved by dealing with me? Dealing with…" he trailed off, gesturing to his entire self with a loose wave of his hand, "…with all this?"

As he'd expected, Agatha's gaze dropped to his chest, where the worst of the damage had been. Agatha had seen the damage, of course. She'd been the one to change the bandages, feed him more laudanum that was good for him because he couldn't stand the pain, and tell him that everything would be alright.

Come to think of it, then, Agatha *had* lied to him before. She'd stroked his hair and told him that it would all be over and he would be himself again soon enough. A lie, plain and simple.

"I think you ought to let her decide for herself," Agatha said at last. "Instead of making up her mind for her. Do you know, Cicero allows her to brush him? She brings pocketfuls of apples and sugar lumps. That horse is going to be too fat to fit in his stall soon enough. He *likes* her, don't you know? That means something. It has to mean something."

Gideon closed his eyes. "I think both of us would prefer for me to keep my distance."

He found himself conjuring up an image of Cicero standing in his stall. The horse didn't like standing still for too long, and Gideon knew in his heart that the horse deserved to gallop free across the fields.

He hadn't galloped for a long time, though. Cicero would remember the movements, wouldn't he?

Cicero, at least, deserves better.

Gideon pinched the bridge of his nose, willing the faint throb of a headache to ease up. What sort of woman spent hours feeding and caring for a horse that would never let her on its back? Cicero was not a *friendly* horse. If he liked her, that said a great deal about the woman herself.

Prudence. I shouldn't keep thinking of her as that woman. *It's hardly respectful.*

"I know you didn't want to marry," Agatha said quietly. "But she's a victim here just as much as you are. Neither of you chose this, but it's happened now. You can shut yourself up in your study and try and ignore everything, or you can make the best of it. Which seems to be the most sensible choice to you?"

Gideon sighed. He did a lot of sighing lately.

Agatha was the sort of woman who believed that one should get *on* with things. Perhaps for some people, that was good advice. Gideon had certainly had it said to him, over and over again, in the weeks and months after he'd returned home. Uncle Bartholomew had said it once or twice, staring helplessly across the table at him, trying in vain to find something which would invigorate Gideon's desire to *live*.

None of it had worked. None of Agatha's firm talks and lectures had worked, and none of his uncle's tricks. Of course, the latest of that trick had left him saddled with a wife, but Gideon was sure that he could just wait a little longer. Prudence would get bored, soon enough. He wasn't mistreating her, he was just showing her that this wasn't the life she wanted. She could have a better life in London, or Derby, or anywhere, really, that wasn't here.

It was for the best. It *was* for the best. Gideon had to keep telling himself that.

Suddenly, his mind conjured up an image of his dining room, with a long, well-polished table. He saw the table was set for one, most of the wooden expanse bare and empty. He saw Prudence sitting there, elbow on the table, chin in her hand, eating mechanically. He saw her stirring her food round her plate, too miserable even to eat.

He bit his lip.

"Is she miserable?"

Agatha blinked at this question. "I never said she was miserable. Just bored."

"Well, I don't want her bothering Cicero."

"I see," Agatha's expression turned neutral, like a shutter had come down. "Well, you can certainly forbid her from going to the stables, if you like."

Gideon rolled his eyes. "I'm not a monster, Agatha. I won't *forbid* her from going anywhere or doing anything. To be frank, I'm not sure that she's the sort of woman who'd listen even if I did. Can't you just find her another occupation? Does she read? Sew? Play the pianoforte?"

"The old piano in the library is very much out of tune, we'll have to hire somebody to look at it before it can be played. She seems to enjoy reading, and already takes books to bed. But not every young woman wants to spend her days shut up in a library reading."

"Why not?"

There was a brief pause. Gideon looked up at Agatha, and she looked back.

"Because not everybody enjoys it," Agatha said heavily, once she seemed to realize that it was a genuine question. "I'm a great advocate of reading, naturally, but sitting inside reading is *not* good for the health. Look at you, young master, with all due respect. Your skin is white as paper. A little sunshine wouldn't go amiss."

He scowled. "I'm quite alright, thank you, Agatha. Can't you find her some other occupation?"

"I've thought about it, but I don't know what to do. She doesn't need to do much with running the household and doesn't seem inclined to bother me about it. Is there something you can suggest?"

He thought for a moment. What *did* young women like to do? Dance, maybe? Well, that was out of the question. There was nobody to dance with. He'd never been much of a dancer, even before his leg was ruined. Go for walks? Throw tea parties? Gideon sank lower in his seat, starting to feel like a silly old man, trying to amuse a small child.

"I don't know what fine ladies like to do with their time," he said at last, vaguely piqued. "Paint, maybe?"

Agatha pursed her lips. "Well, if you joined her for dinner tonight, you might be able to get some suggestions."

"I..."

"I'll set an extra place for you, then, Lord Rycroft."

74

Agatha smiled sweetly, gathering up the tea things and retreating. Gideon was left staring at the closed door, the pie and a cup of tea awaiting him on his desk.

He scowled at the pie. Perhaps it wouldn't be the worst thing in the world if he *did* join her for dinner. It would be better than having all the dishes squashed together on his desk, at any rate. They could engage in polite conversation, she would get extremely bored, and would soon announce that she was packing up and leaving.

Yes, perhaps this was for the best.

Not today, though. Not tonight. He wouldn't join her tonight. Tomorrow, perhaps.

Outside, a shriek caught his attention. Heaving himself to his feet, Gideon limped over to the window. Far below, Prudence stood in the courtyard, with one of the maids. Gideon could never remember their names. Flowers, weren't they? The two women were dipping their fingers in the horse trough and flicking water at each other, squealing and laughing.

Abruptly, Prudence glanced up at the window, as if sensing eyes on her. Gideon drew back behind the curtain, heart thumping. When he gathered his courage enough to glance out again, Prudence was gone, and the courtyard was empty.

Chapter Nine

Prudy had to fight not to go running to the door as soon as she heard the knock. She'd been listening intently for the sound of carriage wheels rumbling up the drive all morning, and now she was *here*. If it hadn't been for the black sky, threatening a storm, and the driving rain, she thought she might actually have gone out and waited on the front step. As she thought of this idea, a blindingly white crack of lightning lit up the sky.

She shivered. The fire was lit, and there were plenty of candles to stave off the darkness, but that didn't really *help*.

One of the unused parlours served as Prudy's personal little room. There was a writing desk for letters – she had plenty of time to write those – and a fireplace, as well as comfortable sofas for lounging around. The windows provided a good view of the front gardens, and it was all Prudy could do not to go and press her nose up against the glass, watching her friend climb out of her carriage. Rain bounced off the well-lacquered surface, and off the curve of the umbrella held up to shield the occupant's well-arranged hair.

Who ever thought I'd be so happy to see Cynthia?

However, at long last, when Rose ushered Cynthia into the little parlour, Cynthia seemed just as happy to see her friend.

"Prudy!" Cynthia cried, holding out her arms. Prudy went rushing over to her, and the two girls hugged each other tight. For once, Cynthia didn't complain about her lace, or her hair, or her silk getting crumpled. They just hugged each other.

"I'll bring tea, shall I?" Rose said, loudly, just the way Agatha had told her *not* to do.

Prudy, chin hooked over Cynthia's shoulder, nodded, and the maid slipped away, closing the door behind her.

At last, the girls released each other. Prudy felt somewhat shaky.

"I'm so glad to see you," Cynthia breathed. "I wanted to come earlier, but Mama said you were newly married and it wasn't proper yet. I thought you wouldn't mind, but I still had to wait."

"I would have loved a visit earlier, but I suppose we should think of the look of the thing. Sit down, sit down."

Cynthia sat, letting out a long, slow sigh. She glanced around the room, eyes wide. She looked nervous, shoulders high and lips pinched. Prudy wondered just what courage her friend had had to summon to come here at all, considering the reputation of the place. She'd half expected Cynthia to politely refuse her invitation.

"It looks so *ordinary* in here. Of course, the hall outside was shockingly big, like a real Gothic abbey, I've never seen anything quite like it... but in here it looks almost ordinary."

"Is that a compliment or an insult?" Prudy asked dryly. "It's a nice enough house, isn't it? Agatha and the maids polished up the floor of the Great Hall especially for your coming. I don't think many guests visit here."

Cynthia winced. "No, I suppose not. Hard to believe you've been married for two *whole weeks*."

Prudy swallowed. *The longest weeks of my life,* she thought, but didn't say it.

"Yes, isn't it? I can't wait to have Catherine to visit. Maybe even my parents, and Blanche."

Cynthia glanced around, as if expecting somebody to be listening from behind the sofa. "And what about *him*? What is he like?"

Prudy hesitated. The simple truth was, she didn't know. The longest conversation she had ever had with her own husband, the longest time they had ever spent together, was when she'd offered herself as a wife instead of Catherine. They exchanged greetings, occasionally, when they passed in the hallways, but that was all. Whole days had gone by without Prudy seeing the man, until she at last asked Agatha if he had left, only to be informed that he was still there. In his study, of course.

Prudy had considered going there, walking right in, sitting down, and asking him why he hated her so much.

She'd never managed it, and it was probably for the best.

And then the memory of that first night came back, when he'd walked in and seen her in the bathtub, and Prudy's face heated. Best not to think of *that* one. That incident certainly did not count.

"I haven't seen him much," she admitted. "He's very busy. He seems pleasant enough."

Cynthia looked a little disappointed. Prudy wondered what she'd expected – tales of cruelty and strange behaviour?

"Oh. Well, you're lucky. I know plenty of married ladies who only wish their husbands would leave them alone. Oh, like Mr and Mrs Thompson – *have* you heard? Oh, it's the most shocking thing..."

Cynthia launched into a piece of Society gossip, and Prudy was able to relax a little.

There was more news, naturally. Prudy might live closer to Dalton Town than Cynthia, but she knew far less about what went on in it. The militia were coming, apparently, and everybody was in a flutter, including Cynthia's troublesome relations. Her younger cousins were putting on too much weight, apparently, and Prudy nodded at that, trying to suppress a yawn.

Cynthia paused, eyeing her narrowly.

"I believe you have lost weight, Prudy."

"Have I?"

"Yes. See how loose that gown is around your waist. You look very well, actually, just take care you don't lose too much."

Prudy glanced down at herself. "Well, I've been helping with the chores."

Cynthia sucked in a breath, eyes wide. "You've been *what*?"

It was a mistake to say that, of course, but too late now.

"Well, it's such a large house," Prudy managed. "There's Agatha, the housekeeper, she does all the cooking. There's Joseph Smith, he does all the gardening and helps care the horse. There are the maids..."

"Only *one* horse?"

"Yes, yes, but that doesn't matter. There are two maids, Daisy and Rose, and they already work so very hard. There's so much cleaning to be done, and Agatha likes everything tidy and neat. I just help them for a few hours a day."

"A few hours!" Cynthia choked. "Goodness, Prudy, you shock me! Don't tell anybody else about that. People will think you've gone mad."

She sniffed, drawing herself up in her seat.

On cue, the door opened, and Rose and Daisy came in, carefully bearing a tray each of tea things. Agatha hovered behind them, on the lookout for spilled tea or dropped crumbs. All conversation stopped while the tea was poured, and when the servants left, they left the door open. Prudy decided to leave it as it was. After all, the open door provided a lovely view of the grand Great Hall.

Cynthia might think she'd gone mad, but there was no denying that this was *Prudy's* home, and it was beautiful.

"So," Cynthia said, after a pause, "have you seen the monster of Rycroft Hall yet? Or the *ghost*? Come to think of it, they might be the same thing. The stories are never clear."

Prudy sighed. "You know I don't believe in that sort of thing, Cynthia."

Even as she spoke, however, Prudy remembered the footsteps she'd heard her first night here. They'd been clear as day, no matter how hard she tried to convince herself they were just a dream. There'd been other noises since then. Nothing quite so clear, just creaks and groans when there should be quiet instead. She didn't much like it, but then, surely old houses did make odd noises at times, didn't they?

"Well, you must believe in the dead animals, at the very least. You know, the ones being found all over the land? It's quite a shocking thing. It *must* be poachers."

Prudy frowned. "I haven't heard anything of the sort. Gideon would have told me," she added, even though of course he wouldn't have done.

Cynthia huffed. "Well, I'm surprised. My uncle is a magistrate, and he said the problem is so bad that they're considering setting watching parties for the poachers."

"But surely, if this is all happening on Gideon's... on *our* land, it's only our concern?"

"My dear, do you never go into town?" Cynthia gave a tittering laugh. "I declare, you're quite uneducated in these matters. The land is Lord Rycroft's, naturally, but there is a well on the land which belongs to the people of Dalton Town, and there's a path they follow to get to it. So, you see, they might encounter poachers on that path, and it would be dangerous."

"I see," Prudy muttered, feeling small and silly. She *ought* to know more about what was happening on her land and in her town. Gideon must know about it, but why hadn't he told her?

That answer came quickly. He didn't tell her because he didn't want to see her. Agatha had set a second place at the dinner table for at least a week, and at first Prudy's heart had leapt. Any company would be excellent, anything that stopped her bothering the poor servants when they were trying to get their work done.

But Gideon had never joined her, and Prudy had given up expecting him to. She wasn't going to tell Cynthia about that, though. It would be all over town, and she would become known as the miserable, sad little bride, unloved, uncared for, ignored.

It smarted, and Prudy pressed her lips together.

I can make this work. I can find a place for myself. I can. I just... just need to persevere. He'll come around, sooner or later. I am Lady Rycroft, after all, and nobody can take that away from me.

Not even Cynthia. Not even him.

"He is kind to you, isn't he?" Cynthia suddenly asked, all in a rush. Prudy glanced at her friend in surprise, and found Cynthia eyeing her anxiously.

It was almost touching.

"He is kind to me," Prudy said.

It wasn't a lie, but not exactly the truth, either. Gideon was simply nothing to her. He didn't go out of his way to make her life unpleasant, but neither did he look at her, or speak to her, or spend time with her.

Perhaps he wanted to marry Catherine after all, Prudy thought, and her gut curdled at that thought. *Maybe if she had become Lady Rycroft, things would be different.*

He doesn't like me.

Cynthia seemed content with that and smiled in relief.

"Oh, that's good, I'm so glad. He is an *odd man*, you know, everybody says it. He shuts himself up here like he's hiding from something. Don't you think so?"

Prudy opened her mouth to say *no*, he was not *hiding,* but was interrupted by a tremendous clap of thunder from outside. She jumped so hard her teacup clattered on its saucer, spilling hot tea over her wrist.

"Oh, goodness," Cynthia laughed. "Do you mean to tell me you're *still* afraid of thunderstorms? After all this time?"

Prudy went bright red. "That's not funny, Cynthia. I..."

She never had the chance to finish her sentence, because there was a second *boom*, much closer this time.

The front door banged open, the wind allowed to catch it and blow it angrily back with a *bang*, making both girls jump this time.

Voices drifted in, and Prudy recognized them both.

"... and the roof is an easy fix," came the low, gruff tones of Joseph Smith, the kindly gardener who'd given her a pot of grease to soften up Cicero's leather bridle and hadn't even looked sideways at her for wanting such a thing. "It's just when we'll get the chance to do it, that's all."

A long sigh followed this statement, and the hairs on Prudy's arms stood up.

"Well, he has to be done as soon as possible, Joseph," Gideon responded. The tip of his cane made a *clacking* sound on the smooth floor. "We can't expect our poor tenants to live in a house with a hole in the..."

His voice faded away as they passed by the open doorway and caught a glimpse of Cynthia and Prudy sitting inside, tea entirely forgotten.

"Lady Rycroft, my apologies," Joseph said at once, bowing nervously. "I didn't realise you had guests, or else we'd have gone around the back."

Both men wore raincoats and hats, water streaming down them to puddle on the floor about their feet. Gideon's gaze landed first on Prudy, then slid along to look at Cynthia, too.

For the first time, it occurred to Prudy that perhaps she ought to have warned her husband she was inviting over a guest.

"You remember Cynthia, don't you, husband?" she managed at last, voice just a little squeaky.

A muscle jumped in Gideon's jaw. With his black raincoat and hair plastered to his forehead with rain, he looked even paler and more ethereal than before.

Handsome, too. Prudy could not deny it – he was a good-looking man, although perhaps not in the showy, preening way that so many Society gentlemen affected. Besides, if she could think *any* man was handsome, it was her husband.

"I remember," he said, after a painfully long pause. "I wasn't aware we were having guests."

"It's just a social call," Prudy said, a trifle desperately. "I should have mentioned. I am sorry."

He blinked at that, some spell broken.

"It hardly matters. Good afternoon to you, Miss Cynthia. And to you… wife."

There was something in the way he said *wife* that felt uneasy, unpractised. He gave a sharp bow, and then both men moved to walk away.

Squelch.

Prudy's gaze dropped, and she saw, for the first time, a perfect imprint of Gideon's boot sole left on the shiny marble floor. Mud caked his boots, and Joseph Smith's, and the two men had left a trail of footprints leading to the front door.

Prudy leapt to her feet with a cry.

"Your boots!"

It was louder than she'd expected, and her voice echoed. The others all froze, staring at her as if she'd gone mad. Prudy cleared her throat, forcing herself to meet Gideon's eye.

"Take off your boots, please," she managed.

"I beg your pardon?" Gideon spluttered. To his credit, Joseph Smith glanced back at his footprints, winced, and immediately began to pull off his boots, creeping away on stockinged feet.

Prudy moved forward a few steps, until she and Gideon were standing close together, either side of the door threshold.

"You've left muddy footprints all over the floor," she said, refusing to drop her gaze. He looked outraged. "Rose and Daisy scrubbed that floor only this morning. Please, take off your boots."

Cynthia gave a choking sort of gasp.

"You want me to take off my boots? In my own Great Hall?" Gideon said, slowly.

Prudy swallowed, tilting up her chin. "Yes, please. They worked so hard on the floor, you see."

He held her gaze for a moment more, and Prudy held her breath.

Then Gideon gave a long, slow sigh, as if he had no energy to fight, and began to toe off his boots. The first came off easily, but he had to lean a little heavier on his cane to take off the other. Bending down, Gideon picked up his dirty boots, muddy water still dripping down, and held them up for her inspection.

"Better?" he asked sardonically.

She refused to bite. "Yes, thank you. I'm sure Agatha will appreciate your consideration."

He held her gaze for at least fifteen minutes longer. Or

perhaps it was only a few heartbeats. However long it was, the tension seemed to last forever.

She could tell, of course, that he was *not* pleased. Wives did not tell their husbands what to do, everybody knew that, even if it was common sense and only fair.

Gideon dropped his gaze first. Grunting, he shook his head and began to pad away down the dark hallway, stockinged feet making hardly any noise on the floor.

Prudy watched him go, not sure what to make of the odd, tingling feeling inside her chest, coiling and tightening. It was like the feeling of nerves, only different.

She closed the door and leaned against it, turning back to her friend.

"You can't do that!" Cynthia burst out.

"Can't do what?"

"A gentleman can wear his boots in his own house if he likes!"

"Normally, I would have no objection. But you saw the state of his boots. He'd already walked mud halfway across the floor. As I said, the maids had just scrubbed it."

Cynthia sniffed disdainfully. "Well, they would just scrub it again. That's what they're here for."

Prudy shrugged, sitting down beside her friend. She felt oddly shaky. At least Gideon hadn't ignored her – Cynthia would have told everybody.

"I think he likes you very much," Cynthia said abruptly, causing Prudy to choke on her tea.

"I *beg* your pardon?"

A light flush had risen to Cynthia's cheeks. "You heard me. He likes you, I'm sure of it. What happiness for you."

"He does not *like me*, Cynthia. I irritate him. The truth is, he mostly avoids me, when he can. He wants us to lead separate lives. He didn't *want* to marry. This was a marriage of convenience, and everybody knows we were both strong-armed into it."

Cynthia eyed her for a long moment.

"If you say so," she said at last. "Now, are you going to cut this divine-looking sponge cake, or am I? I'm fairly starving after all that excitement."

Chapter Ten

There was really no getting around the fact she *was* here, and for the time being, the wretched girl was going nowhere.

Oh, Gideon had tried to pretend his new wife did not exist, but it was frankly impossible. There were bits of her everywhere – ladies' clothes hanging up on the washing line, which he could see from his bedroom window, new books signed out of the library (he supposed he should be grateful she even *used* the sign-in, sign-out sheet), curtains opened when he'd left them closed, and so on.

And, of course, there was *her*. When he climbed the stairs to bed at night, he could glance along the hallway to the other wing and see a line of light coming out from under her bedroom door. He ran into her all the time, along the hallways and in the Great Hall.

And, of course, there'd been the bathtub incident – he still cringed to recall himself barging into her *washroom* like that – and more recently, the boots incident.

Gideon wished he'd known that the girl was going to bring one of her wretched friends here. It was to be expected, she could hardly shut herself up like a recluse for the rest of her life...

Like you do.

... but really, he'd hoped that she would *leave* before she started inviting people over.

Gideon groaned aloud. He was standing outside the closed dining room door, wearing a stiff, uncomfortable evening suit, and a waistcoat in an uncomfortably gaudy shade of pale jade.

Don't be such a coward. Just go on in there. You can't eat hunched over at your desk forever, after all.

He breathed in and out, concentrating on the feel of breath leaving his lungs and filling them again. It was a trick he'd learned from one of the army surgeons, to calm one's mind and soothe away anxieties. It worked fairly well, most of the time. Not all the time, of course.

Before he could give himself a chance to change his mind, Gideon turned the doorknob and walked in.

The table was set for dinner, of course, a good three-quarters of it left bare. The remaining quarter was set with silver dishes and cutlery, a candelabra burning wastefully away in the centre of it all, despite the countless candles lit along the sides of the room, *and* the fire.

Gideon's wife sat at the head of the table, propping up her head on her palm, drawing figure-eights in her soup with a spoon. She glanced idly up when the door opened, and when she saw who was entering, she dropped the spoon with a *clatter*, scattering soup everywhere.

"Lord Rycroft!" she gasped. "That is, *Gideon*. What are you doing here?"

Just get into the room. Sit down, just sit down.

"What do you think I'm doing?" he shot back. "There's a place set for me, isn't there?"

That part was certainly true – Agatha had dutifully set two places at the table almost since the day Prudence had arrived.

Prudence cleared her throat, fishing for the spoon. There were no servants to wait on her, Gideon noticed. He was relieved at that. He himself had never much liked having somebody stand over him when he was eating, and perhaps she shared his feelings on that matter.

Gideon stalked over to the table, keen to sit down before he did something embarrassing like hobble out of the room again. His leg was exceptionally bad today, and he was forced to lean heavily on his cane. Cold, wet weather was always the worst. He could feel the scars on his body throb and ache, mapping out a trail of destruction from his leg all the way to his jaw.

He sat down with a thump and began to busy himself with spooning out some soup.

And then the silence landed, like a heavy blanket. A blanket of snow, maybe, thick and dense and icy cold.

Gideon generally enjoyed silence. For him, quiet was synonymous with peace, and he had plenty of it in his study.

There was something different about this silence. It was taut and uncomfortable and was often broken by the muffled sounds of eating, or the clang of cutlery on crockery.

You're not a child, Gideon thought angrily. *Say something to her. Anything will do.*

I'm sorry I saw you in the bathtub.

No, no, not that! Anything but that!

It was too late, of course. The image that Gideon had worked so hard to banish had resurfaced. Prudence sat in the big copper bathtub, eyes wide with shock, the pale, white skin of her shoulders rising above the water, steam curling around her, hair sticking to her forehead and neck.

He cleared his throat.

"Prudence, I think..."

She began talking at the exact same time. "Perhaps we..."

They both broke off abruptly, and there was more of that uneasy silence. This time, Prudence managed to speak first.

"Prudy."

He blinked. "I beg your pardon?"

"Call me Prudy," she said firmly, meeting his eye. "I hate *Prudence*. I'm not a particularly prudent person at the best of times, so the name doesn't fit anyway. My sister always called me Prudy, and I like that name. Call me Prudy, please."

Gideon bit his lip. "Very well, if that's what you would prefer."

She let out a breath. "Thank you. Well, I'm glad you're here, because I think I owe you an apology."

He lifted an eyebrow. Well, *this* was unexpected. "You do?"

"I do," she responded, visibly steeling herself. "Gideon, I am sorry I shouted at you for wearing your boots across Agatha's clean floor. While I don't regret you taking them off, I shouldn't have scolded you, certainly not in front of Joseph and my guest. It was wrong of me. I have a great deal to know about being a supportive spouse, and I hope you'll forgive me."

Gideon cleared his throat, dropping his gaze to the murky green surface of his soup. Was this pea soup? He hated pea soup.

"There's really nothing to forgive," he answered at last. "Perhaps you *were* a little sharp, but I ought to have seen the clean floor and taken off my boots at the door. It was thoughtless of me."

She blinked at him, as if having difficulty understanding what he'd said.

"Oh," she managed at last. "Well, thank you for being so honest."

"It's quite alright."

And then the silence was back. Gideon, not used to having

an audience for his meals, accidentally slurped his soup, wincing at his own clumsiness. Prudence pretended not to notice.

Prudy, he corrected himself. *Call her Prudy.*

"Did you have a good time with your friend today?" Gideon managed at last.

Prudy cleared her throat, shifting in her seat. "I did, yes. And I am sorry I didn't tell you she was coming. I… I didn't really think. At home, I could invite my friends over whenever I liked and my parents didn't much care."

"Well, I don't expect you to ask permission here. This is your home, too."

What are you doing? Gideon asked himself fiercely. *You don't* want *her to make this her home. You want her to leave, remember? It's the best for everybody!*

But the words were said, and he couldn't go back and unsay them now.

When he dragged his gaze up from his soup bowl, he saw Prudy staring at him, a strange expression in her eyes. A tingle ran down his spine, not unpleasant, but not something he *wanted* to feel. Clearing his throat again, Gideon directed his eye back down at his soup bowl.

"Thank you," Prudy said, voice soft. "That means a great deal to me. I know this… this *situation* is not what either of us would have wanted, but I believe we can make the best of it."

She reached for a glass of wine, holding it up. It took Gideon far too long to realize she was proposing a toast.

"To making the best of it," she said, smiling wryly.

"To making the best of it," he echoed, and took a sip. It was good wine. Probably one of his best wines from the cellar. Gideon sighed. Oh well. No sense in letting them rot, was there?

"Cynthia was full of gossip from the town," Prudy continued, seeming to grow in confidence now. "She said that the militia are coming to town."

Gideon's fingers tightened around his spoon. "Oh?" he said lightly, praying that the subject would change.

"Yes, apparently everybody is fluttering in excitement."

His knuckles stood out white. "Excited? Whatever for?"

"For the militia, of course! Everybody loves a redcoat."

The stem of the silver spoon was now digging painfully into

Gideon's palm, and he forced himself to release it. A vivid line stood out on his skin. He flexed his fingers, not daring to glance at Prudy.

She was sipping her soup again, unaware.

"Apparently there's going to be all kinds of balls and whatnot. Everybody is talking about it."

"They're fools," Gideon spat, before he could stop himself.

Well, that got her attention. Prudy glanced at him, eyes wide with surprise.

"What do you mean?"

He swallowed hard. "What do you think I mean? I hate all this nonsensical fluttering around the militia. They're soldiers, for heaven's sake. Soldiers are not entertainment, and war is not a parade."

"Goodness," Prudy remarked dryly, "Aren't you serious? Why can't people find a little joy in their days? There's no harm in it."

"If there is, the people fluttering around *redcoats* won't see that harm."

She sighed. "I don't think that there's any harm in telling a man he looks handsome in uniform."

Gideon slammed his hand down on the table. "Is that all you think it is? Looking handsome? A *uniform*? You're a greater fool than I thought."

Prudy eyed him back, unimpressed. "Tell me, Gideon, do you hate *any* kind of enjoyment, or just when we're talking?"

"Don't make this about me."

"There's only two of us in the room, Gideon. Who should it be about?"

"Oh, for heaven's sake. Let's just eat."

He picked up his spoon again, but his hand shook too badly to try and scoop up any soup, even if his appetite would allow him to try.

Calm, calm, man, Gideon soothed himself, ignoring the regular throb of pain through his body. *Breathe in, slowly. Count. Hold the breath, count. Let it out, long and slow. Concentrate on the rhythm of your breathing. Nothing else matters.*

Prudy sighed, taking another sip of wine. "Fine, fine. Although, for what it's worth, I think *you* would look remarkably

89

good in uniform."

It was too much.

Gideon leapt to his feet, the chair screeching backwards and toppling over with a tremendous crash. His bad leg half-buckled, and he lurched forward, barely saving himself from crumpling. He knocked the table, and the cutlery clattered loudly. Soup slopped over the edge of his bowl, and his wine glass, hardly touched, fell over altogether. A pool of red wine, vivid as blood in the candlelight, spread slowly over the fine white tablecloth. In a minute, it would drip over the edge of the table and stain the carpet, too.

Gideon felt sick.

Prudy was staring at him, soup and wine forgotten.

"Gideon?" she began hesitantly, but he didn't let her finish. There were running footsteps along the hall. Agatha, no doubt, hearing the commotion. She wouldn't come bursting in, but he didn't particularly want Agatha to see him at the moment.

Gideon knew he must look a sight. White-faced, eyes glittering, spots of colour dancing in his cheeks as if he had a fever. His face would be twisted with pain, body sagging drunkenly to one side.

Pathetic.

"You are a stupid little girl," he snarled. Prudy flinched backwards.

"Gideon, I didn't mean…"

"You don't understand anything, do you? You don't *care* to understand. You're just talking and talking, and none of it means anything, and yet you expect me to sit and listen to all this… all this nonsense. Well, I won't. I can't."

"Gideon…"

Wide-eyed, Prudy reached forward as if to take his hand, but Gideon twisted his arm away, very nearly overbalancing as he did so. He stumbled backwards, snatching his cane, and limped out of the dining room as fast as his bad leg could do so.

The hallway outside the dining room was dark after the brightness inside, and Gideon stood for a moment, blinking in the gloom.

"Lord Rycroft?"

Agatha, of course. Gideon closed his eyes. He could see

nothing except Prudy, sitting at the table, looking up at him, eyes wide and face taut with hurt. He heard his own voice, pitching to a shout, ringing in his ears.

"Some wine was spilt in there," Gideon heard himself say. "Could you clean it up, please?"

***

Coward. Coward. Coward.

Gritting his teeth against the pain – Gideon had knocked his leg against the dining table, it seemed, and the familiar ache had sharpened to something with teeth, climbing up his leg and coiling around his hip – he limped down the hallway.

It was close to eleven o' clock at night, and Gideon had had hours to rehearse what he wanted to say.

Prudy, I am sorry about my behaviour earlier. It's no excuse, but I was in terrible pain. I am sorry I shouted and spoke to you the way I did. Could you forgive me?

An explanation. She would require an explanation. Gideon sighed.

When you said what you did about the militia, it upset me because... because...

The words wouldn't come. Gideon reached the landing at the top of the stairs, where the hallways diverged, and he had absolutely no idea what to say. He could see a line of light coming out from under Prudy's room.

I'll start with a plain 'I'm sorry', he decided.

Limping down the hallway, Gideon noticed that the faint line of light was much thicker than usual. In fact, the door was slightly ajar.

"Prudence?" he asked warily. "Prudy?"

There was no response, and he gingerly pushed open the door.

The fire was dying down in the hearth, and a few candles lit up the room. The bedclothes were turned down, and a steaming cup of tea sat on the nightstand. However, the bedroom was clearly empty.

Gideon hovered in the doorway for a moment, uncertain.

There were plenty of reasons why Prudy could have left her

91

room at this time of night. To fetch a book, perhaps, or to get a late-night slice of cake. But all of Gideon's imaginings had centred on being able to knock on the door and immediately come face to face with her. After that, he was sure, the apology would spill out all by itself.

Should I go in and wait? What if she's still angry with me?

And then he heard voices and muted laughter from the staircase. He made out Prudy's voice and then Agatha's, discussing the second volume of some novel or another.

Gideon's chest tightened. Did he want to make his apology in front of Agatha, who'd heard everything he said in the dining room, and would look at him with that disappointed expression?

What if Prudy didn't forgive him? What if she thought that him coming here, to her room, was overstepping?

It was too much. They were already at the landing.

Turning tail, Gideon limped away down the hallway as fast as his bad leg could carry him.

I'll apologise another time, he thought, shame curdling in his gut. *There'll be more opportunities.*

Chapter Eleven

"I can't believe I've never made bread before."

Agatha chuckled. "Well, I never thought I'd hear a lady so excited to knead her own bread. I thought I was dreaming when you came in and asked, let me tell you. You're a quick study, Lady Rycroft, and no mistake."

It still felt odd to be called *Lady Rycroft*, but somehow it felt less strange when she had an apron on and flour up to her elbows. Prudy shot a quick, grateful look at the older woman. Agatha's gaze was fixed on the knot of dough, which was gradually taking shape under Prudy's floury hands.

Of course, Agatha had heard the argument between Gideon and Prudy last night. No sooner had Gideon stormed out, letting the door swing behind him, than Agatha came quietly in, and began mopping up the growing puddle of wine on the table.

They hadn't talked about it, of course, and for that Prudy was grateful. Gideon's words still stung.

You are a stupid little girl. You don't understand anything, do you? You don't care to understand. You're just talking and talking, and none of it means anything, and yet you expect me to sit and listen to all this... all this nonsense. Well, I won't. I can't.

A stupid little girl. Well, Prudy had never expected to hear her husband say such a thing. He'd meant it, too, she'd seen it on his face.

She'd gone over their conversation again and again to try and figure out what had upset him so much. It had something to do with the militia. Perhaps he truly thought all the fluttering over the soldiers *was* silly, but shouldn't that have occasioned an eye roll and a few sharp words, not... not *that*?

Prudy was angry, of course, blisteringly so, but she also felt ashamed for some reason. He'd made an effort. He'd joined her, even tried to make small talk, then she'd misstepped somewhere and sent him fleeing away.

It's like trying to lure a wild deer out of the undergrowth.

A haughty, unpleasant wild deer, who thinks I'm a silly little gossip and doesn't want to come out of the undergrowth.

She put her weight behind the knead, a trifle vengefully.

"That looks good enough, Lady Rycroft. Now, we'll put it back in the pot, and let it set for half an hour more before it goes into the oven."

Prudy stopped kneading, wiping knots of dried dough and flour off her fingers. There was certainly a satisfaction to be had in baking something for oneself. Agatha had watched her every step of the way, of course, but Prudy had made that dough all by herself.

"I'm afraid that it'll be cold meats and cheese for dinner tonight," Agatha said, draping a clean strip of muslin over the pot to cover the dough. "It's my granddaughter's birthday today. I'm going to their house to celebrate, and Joseph's escorting me there. I'll likely stay overnight. I know I ought to have asked your permission, but Lord Rycroft says that I can go to visit family whenever I like."

"Oh, you had no need to ask," Prudy said at once. "I hope you have a wonderful time. Do you have a present for your granddaughter?"

"Besides a few tarts, no."

"Ah, then you must help yourself to something to my trinket box. I have plenty of ribbons I've never used, would she like one of those?"

Agatha flushed. "I'm sure she would, Lady Rycroft. Are you sure you wouldn't mind?"

"Of course not," Prudy reassured her, washing her hands in the bowl. Thank goodness Agatha had insisted on the apron – she had gotten flour *everywhere*. "Choose whatever colour your granddaughter would like."

"Well, that's kind, Lady Rycroft, thank you. I should warn you, Rose and Daisy go home on weekends. They're meant to stay if Joseph and I are gone, but I never have the heart to make them. Will you mind being in the house alone?"

Prudy would very much mind that, but what was she meant to do? Force the maids to stay? Tell Agatha to miss her granddaughter's birthday?

Mama would.

"Of course I don't mind," Prudy lied smoothly. "I hope you all have a wonderful night, to be sure."

She was saved from further deception – because Agatha did

not seem convinced – by Joseph himself clumping into the kitchen. Despite the early hour, he looked tired.

"Is he back?" Agatha asked at once.

"Aye, just walked in now," Joseph answered, helping himself to some tea.

"Who?" Prudy asked. "Are you talking about Gideon? Where could Lord Rycroft have gone, so early in the morning?"

Agatha and Joseph glanced briefly at each other. Joseph's eyebrow flickered, questioningly, and Agatha gave the tiniest of nods. Joseph turned to Prudy, and she guessed that she'd passed some sort of test.

"Lord Rycroft walks around during the night," Joseph answered bluntly. "Hours and hours he walks around, in all weathers. Through the grounds, through the forest, everywhere. Tireless, he is."

Prudy frowned. A prickle ran down her spine, and something stirred at the back of her head. Something that ought to be connecting in her mind but was resolutely *not* doing so.

"Isn't that dangerous?"

Agatha shrugged. "He takes a rifle, just in case. It's not as if we have bears and wolves roaming around in this part of the world."

Prudy couldn't fathom walking out into that pitch blackness, certainly not *voluntarily*, with a warm bed and a crackling fireplace waiting for you at home. Even after several weeks, the absolute darkness of the countryside still gave her the shivers. She missed seeing the bright windows of her neighbours, and the buttery glow of the new streetlamps some places had.

It was comforting. Here, however, there was not only darkness but silence as well. What Prudy wouldn't give for the rattle of carriage wheels on cobbles at an unseemly hour of the night.

"Well, when does he sleep?" she asked at last.

Agatha bit her lip. "I'm not sure he does."

Prudy paused, still washing her hands. "What? Of course he sleeps. Why wouldn't he sleep?"

Agatha suddenly seemed very interested in wiping down the floury surface of the counter. Joseph inspected the toes of his boots.

95

"Well, I don't rightly know," Agatha managed at last, when it was clear that Joseph would rather die than speak. "But I know he doesn't sleep much. Not much at all."

That was not, of course, an answer to Prudy's question, but she suspected that she wasn't going to get an answer to that question. Whatever secret Gideon was keeping, the faithful Agatha and Joseph were going to help him keep it. Prudy had no inclination to pry more than she should.

"Well," Prudy said at last, when the silence got a little too heavy, "I can't wait for this bread. Did you hear, Joseph? I'm baking my own bread today."

"She's got a knack for it," Agatha added, with no small amount of pride.

"Ah, is that so, Lady Rycroft? Well, then, I hope I might be so bold as to request a slice when it's cooked," Joseph asked, grinning.

"It would be my honour," Prudy replied with a laugh. And for a moment, in that warm, delicious-smelling kitchen, she forgot all about her troubles and the man she was married to, along with the strange feeling in the pit of her stomach which was something like excitement and something like unease, and entirely unfamiliar into the bargain.

Almost.

***

Prudy put aside the book with a shudder.

"That," she said to the grey cat curled up beside her, "was a mistake. What was I thinking, reading Mrs Radcliffe on a night like tonight? When I'm alone in the house, no less?"

Not entirely alone, her brain reminded her, but Prudy did her best to ignore it.

The cat – a kitchen cat, kept to hunt mice – stretched out his paws and yawned. Silly thought it was, Prudy was glad of its company.

Outside, night had closed in. Agatha and Joseph had been gone for hours, and there was nobody in the kitchen.

Just me and the castle of Udolpho. Oh, and Emily St. Aubert, if she'd ever stop fainting, Prudy thought wistfully, reaching out to smooth the cat's warm fur.

It was odd, being so alone, especially in a house as large as this. Back home, there was always somebody around, even if you weren't in the same room together. There were servants, *always* – they weren't allowed afternoons and evenings off, the day the servants here had.

Of course, Prudy liked the servants here a great deal more than the ones at home. Agatha and Joseph were so kind, and Rose and Daisy almost felt like friends rather than maids.

She wasn't *really* alone, not with Gideon in the house.

Although perhaps he's left for his late-night walk, Prudy thought, glancing out of the window. It wasn't raining tonight, but the wind was getting up. She could see the silhouette of trees shifting against the paler sky, moon glittering above it all.

It is pretty, she acknowledged, *so long as you're safe and warm inside. I'd hate to be out on a night like this. Although, who* would *choose to go outside, besides my mad husband? Well, I suppose those poaching watcher groups...*

She stopped dead, sitting bolt upright with a cry that made the grey cat miaow angrily at the disturbance.

Gideon went on late-night walks, alone, with a rifle. Watchers were going out at night to try and catch a poacher.

They'll think he's a poacher.

The idea had unsettled Prudy, no matter how firmly she tried to tell herself it was silly. She got to her feet, pacing up and down the parlour, and eventually went to the window and tried to peer out.

It's bad weather. He won't have gone out.

They won't just shoot on sight, that's nonsense. Why would they do that? They'll ask who it is, and once they know it's Gideon, they'll let him go.

None of it worked to smooth out her worries. Prudy's heart was thumping hard against the inside of her ribcage. She cursed herself for not putting two and two together earlier, and mentioning something to Agatha and Joseph, who almost certainly would have warned *Gideon* about it.

I should warn him myself.

Hitching up her skirts, Prudy shouldered open the door and went racing off into the dark depths of the house.

As she ran, she thought belatedly that Agatha was right about the candles. It *was* a waste to have so many of them around. Dozens of candles had been employed to light up the Great Hall and the surrounding corridors, and they did hardly any good. They might as well save the wax.

As far as Prudy could tell from the little she'd seen of Gideon's habits, he would be in one of two places. His study, or his bedroom upstairs.

She went to the study first, and heart leapt to see light coming in from under the door. She was destined to be disappointed.

Prudy pushed open the door without even bothering to knock, and her heart sank.

A candle was burning low on the desk. The remains of a tea tray sat on the desk, tea long since gone cold. There was no sign of Gideon.

A miaow at her heels made her jump, and the grey cat twined around her ankles.

"Maybe he's gone to bed early," Prudy said uncertainly. "We should check."

The cat pranced at her heels as Prudy raced along hallways and up the stairs, heart pounding. She saw no light coming along the corridor and knew immediately that Gideon was not in his room.

She opened the door, eyes adjusting to the gloom.

He had a neat room, smaller than she might have expected, almost spartan in its decoration. There were no pictures on the walls, plain curtains hung at the window, and everything was immaculately neat. A pile of clothes, perfectly pressed, stood at the end of the bed.

The bed, of course, was tucked in and smoothed out with military precision. In fact, not a single thing was out of place in the room. Prudy winced, conjuring up an image of her room, with crumpled blankets and tossed pillows everywhere, trinkets and clothes tossed carelessly around. Rose and Daisy had more important things to do than tidy Prudy's room, as she'd told them, but perhaps *she* should tidy up a little more. Gideon would probably die of apoplexy if he walked in her room at that moment.

The cat prowled past her, jumping up onto the bed and nosing at the immaculate pile of clothes.

"Get down, get down," Prudy hissed, chasing the cat away. "If that pile falls over, I'll never get it folded perfectly again. He'll know I was snooping."

Not at all offended, the cat sat back on its haunches and eyed her curiously, tail twitching. Prudy ran a nervous hand through her hair, fingers catching on tangles.

"He must have gone out," she said aloud to nobody in particular. Perhaps she was speaking to the cat. "He's gone out, but maybe he'll stick to the grounds, and not go walking about in the forest. I'm sure the watchers won't just shoot indiscriminately. He'll be back any minute, probably."

A knot of tension tightened in Prudy's chest, so intense that she couldn't breathe. The dark room swayed a little, and she forced herself to stagger over to the window. There wasn't much to see, beyond the courtyard below, and the treeline in the distance.

What sort of man walks around in the forest all night, alone? That isn't normal. Nothing about this situation or that wretched man is normal.

For a few minutes, the only sound was Prudy's blood pounding in her ears. On impulse, she wrestled open the window and leaned out, hoping to hear the tap of a cane tip on cobbles, or perhaps a whistle, or perhaps some footsteps.

She held her breath.

And then, quite without warning, a single gunshot rang out, splitting the night air.

Prudy screamed.

Chapter Twelve

The cat went racing out into the night, past Prudy and through the open door.

The wind was colder than Prudy could have imagined, even with the oversized raincoat she wore and the thick rubber boots. Her hands shook when she tied up the laces. There had been a lantern by the door, and it gave off enough light to see by, although not enough to reassure Prudy.

There'd been no further noise beyond the gunshot, except perhaps some muffled shouts which had long since died away. She was trying not to think about it.

There are a hundred reasons for that gunshot, she reminded herself, winding a scarf around her neck. *A real poacher, for example. Oh, how I wish just one person was in the house with me!*

But, as Agatha had said more than once since Prudy had arrived, if wishes were fish nobody would be hungry, and so there was no point in hoping things were otherwise.

Gritting her teeth, Prudy picked up the lantern and stepped out into the night, pulling the door closed behind her.

At once, the wind whipped around her, painfully cold, and she tasted rain and maybe even snow on the air. The lantern rocked, but the glass panels were firm and the flame did not go out. Prudy forced herself to walk forward, away from the (relative) safety of the house and into the dark.

I don't even know where I'm going, she thought bleakly. *What if they think I'm a poacher, too?*

It occurred to Prudy then that perhaps having a group of men from the village – who were probably drunk – wandering around the forest at night, armed, ready to shoot anyone they thought of as a poacher was possibly a bad idea.

"Gideon?" she called, voice weak and a little pathetic against the roar of the wind. "Gideon, are you out there?"

No answer. Prudy scuttled forward, ducking her head against the wind. A few ice-cold smatterings of rain were coming down now, and she suspected a heavy shower was about to follow. Her lantern gave out a small circle of light, but really did very little against the taut darkness. She could make out the shapes of trees and bushes, swaying in the wind, and relied heavily on the worn-down path beneath her boots.

And then, abruptly, the path ended, and she was facing the treeline.

The forest was blacker than pitch, darker and more dense than Prudy could have imagined. She'd gone through this forest, of course, but only ever in the daylight hours, and once on the back of a horse with Patrick Devin, following a neat little path.

It was something else entirely now.

Cringing, Prudy backed away.

"Gideon?" She cried again, voice already getting hoarse. "Gideon, if you can hear me, please answer!"

Was that an answering moan? She held her breath, listening, but the wind squealed and drowned out all other sounds. Turning her back on the forest, Prudy squinted through the dark.

There… there! A low grey wall rounded part of the garden, glinting in the moonlight, and a crumpled dark shape stirred against it.

Prudy didn't wait to think about intruders or even wild animals. She raced towards the shape; skirts hitched up around her knees in a horrifyingly unladylike manner.

The shape resolved itself into a man, and when she held up the lantern, Gideon's rain-soaked face looked up, hair jet black and plastered to his head. His skin was even paler than usual, one hand pressed tight against his shoulder. Dark liquid leaked out from between his fingers, and with a shudder, Prudy realized that it was blood.

"You're shot," she said bluntly.

"What are you doing out here?" Gideon rasped. His voice was tight with pain. "I could hear you shouting."

"I heard a shot. I thought you might have been hurt, and I was right, as it turned out. Come, we must get you inside right away."

He opened his mouth as if he planned to argue, then firmly shut it again.

"Can you help me get inside? Or fetch somebody who can?" he asked eventually.

"I'll help you. Here, give me your arm – your good one – and try and get to your feet. Lean on me, and we'll walk back together."

He was heavier than Prudy had expected, and his bad leg would support little weight. There was no sign of Gideon's cane, or his rifle, if he'd had one. He had no hat, either so she assumed it had been blown away. That meant that his hair was soaking wet, water dripping down into his collar. Prudy could feel how wet his clothes were, and Gideon shivered uncontrollably against her.

"There's a fire in my parlour," Prudy said, teeth gritted against the strain. She wished she'd changed into breeches, as her wet skirts kept tangling around her legs. "You can warm up there."

He said nothing, and Prudy decided to conserve her breath, concentrating on getting home.

When they finally tumbled in through the front door, she felt ready to collapse with exhaustion. Naturally, though, her work was not done. Gideon had to be supported into the parlour, and weakly mumbled something about his study.

"You're not going into your study," she said firmly. "It's cold in there, and there's nowhere to lie down."

He gave up protesting when they crossed the threshold of her parlour, and the warmth of the fire washed over them. Prudy manhandled Gideon down onto a chaise longue, managing to rather deftly strip him out of his coat as she did so. He was wearing a plain black waistcoat and white shirt underneath, which was damp in places but not as wet as she'd feared.

"What are you doing?" Gideon mumbled; eyes glazed.

"What do you think I'm doing?" she retorted, untying his cravat. When she pulled the material away, exposing a triangle of skin at his collar, Gideon's eyes sharpened.

"That's quite enough, thank you," he snapped, trying and failing to sit up. She could see the bullet wound now, red staining the sleeve of his shirt. His hand was soaked in blood where he'd tried to staunch the bleeding, and some of it had even gotten on Prudy.

She was secretly a little proud of herself for not being silly about it. Blanche claimed to have once seen her cousin shoot himself through the foot at a hunting party, and had promptly fainted. Prudy was not particularly enjoying the sight of blood, but neither did she feel weak at the knees.

"We need to summon a doctor," she heard herself say.

"There's no need for that," Gideon shot back. "The bullet went straight through. I've been lucky. The wound needs to be cleaned and sewn up, and that's all I require."

"And how would you know? Have you seen many bullet wounds before?"

"More than you, I can assure you," he retorted, teeth clenched. "Go fetch Agatha. She'll sew it up and clean the wound. No need to concern yourself further."

Prudy crossed her arms. "Agatha isn't here. None of them are. It's just you and I in the house tonight."

If possible, Gideon's face paled even further.

"Oh," he managed. "Oh, dear. You can't fetch a doctor, not without a horse, and Cicero would never let you ride him."

"No, but I'm sure I can sew up your wound," Prudy said, with far more confidence than she felt.

There was a brief silence.

"You?" he echoed, looking more green than white now.

Prudy tossed her head. "Indeed, I. Unless you plan to bleed to death overnight. You can't very well sew up your own wound, can you?"

He squeezed his eyes closed.

"No," Gideon said, after an interminable pause. "I can't. You will have to help me, Prudy."

She let out a long breath. "And I am going to help you, I promise. I warn you, my embroidery is not *accomplished*, and my needlework is not *excellent.*"

He smiled wryly at that, eyes still closed. "I can assure you, Prudy, I don't mind a scar or two. *Pretty* is something lost a long time ago for me."

"Good. Then tell me what to do."

***

Fifteen minutes later, everything was ready. A bowl of boiling water to sterilize the needle and thread, a pair of sharp scissors, and a half bottle of whiskey.

Prudy watched Gideon snatch the whiskey and take a long pull of it.

"I thought that was for sterilizing the wound," she observed.

103

He winced. "It is. It's also to calm my nerves."

"I would argue that *my* nerves want calming more than yours," she remarked, snatching the bottle from him. "It's my hand that needs to hold steady, after all."

"Fair."

Prudy took a mouthful of the whiskey and swirled it experimentally around her mouth.

Ladies did not, of course, drink spirits like whiskey and brandy, and Prudy never had. It tasted truly awful and burned when she finally forced herself to swallow it. She couldn't stop herself pulling a face when it went down, and Gideon chuckled weakly.

"Hold on to that amusement," she said pointedly, threading the needle. Her hands were clean, after Gideon insisted that she scrub them for at least five minutes. "You'll need it."

He had begrudgingly let her remove the waistcoat but refused to take off his shirt. Prudy unlaced a few inches at the neckline, enough to pull down the shirt around his shoulder, revealing the wound. The first thing Prudy noticed, once the blood had been cleaned from the surrounding area, were the scars.

Raised, white and pink scars criss-crossed Gideon's shoulder, peeking out from the folds of his shirt. There was hardly an inch of smooth skin to be seen. She spotted more pockmarks, just like the ones on his face and neck, trailing down his chest, growing thicker and deeper until they looked less like silvery freckles and more like gouges.

"I must say," Gideon said, eyes squeezed closed as she dabbed a whiskey-soaked cloth around the wound, "I thought you'd be more squeamish than this."

"Do you know, so did I. I suppose all that novel-reading and Mrs Radcliffe has desensitized me to horror. Now, are you going to tell me what on earth happened here?"

The wound was clean, so there was nothing for it but for Prudy to pick up her needle and thread and get to her grisly work. For a full moment, perhaps two, there was deathly silence. She was sure they were both holding their breaths.

It's not at all like stitching linen.

"I believe they were a pack of men hunting poachers," Gideon said at last, voice faint. "They stumbled upon me and naturally assumed I was a poacher. I had no lantern or light, so they didn't know who I was."

"So, they just fired a gun at you?" Prudy responded angrily. "Just shot a gun in the dark? Idiots."

"Yes, it was foolish of them," he acknowledged. "I didn't think of that at the time. I concentrated mostly on running away, half afraid I'd get another shot in my back."

The idea of Gideon, face down in the forest with a gunshot wound in his back, still as death, made Prudy shudder uncontrollably. She pulled the thread a trifle too taut, and Gideon winced.

"Sorry," she answered automatically.

"It's fine, you're doing very well," he said, twisting his head to get a look at her handiwork. "A lot less scolding than Agatha, too."

"Does this happen a lot, then?" she enquired, shooting a glance up at his face. His expression was tight with pain, as was to be expected, but it was odd to see him with his eyes closed like this, almost like he was sleeping. There was a peacefulness to his profile, an expression that tugged at something in Prudy's chest.

She averted her gaze to the wound instead.

"Not very often," Gideon said, eyes still closed. "I was in quite a state after the war, though. Agatha had to patch me up frequently."

His muscles tensed at the mention of war, and Prudy – in a rare burst of real prudence – decided not to push the issue.

"Why didn't you call out to the men and tell them who you were?" she asked, snipping off the end of the thread. The front part was sewn up well enough, if somewhat clumsily, and now she would need to do the same on the back. "They might have taken you to a surgeon."

For a moment or two, Gideon didn't respond. He rolled half onto his side, giving Prudy access to the wound on his back. She saw more thickened scar tissue here, too. Some scars seemed to be burns, others long-healed gashes.

Concentrate on the work, Prudy.

"I thought of that," Gideon said at last, long after she'd given up hope of him responding. "But I already have a somewhat... somewhat *macabre* reputation in this town. I thought that being

105

caught wandering around the woods in the dark might not help matters."

"I suppose so," Prudy acknowledged. "It *is* a strange thing to do, but that's your business, and I shall mind my own."

He made a curious huffing noise that *might* have been a chuckle, Prudy wasn't sure. Maybe. Maybe not.

"Besides," he continued, voice tightening as Prudy began to sew again. She was really getting the knack of this now. "The locals use that well very often. I don't want them to feel uncomfortable, and decide to stop using it, as well they might if news of a madman wandering the forests gets around. Without that well, they'll go back to drinking from the river, and there's run-off from the churchyard in it."

"And that is... a bad thing?"

"Some studies believe so, yes," he answered cryptically. "So, that was why I decided to run home instead of asking for help. I thought I'd have more strength. I forget all too often than I'm a cripple now. I lost my walking stick, too."

Prudy bit her lip. "You're too hard on yourself. You ran for goodness knows how long..."

"Limped, rather."

"Well, you still did it, in the freezing rain, in the dark, with a nasty bullet wound in your shoulder. It's impressive."

He twisted to look over his shoulder, eyes shadowy. "And you are impressed, *Prudence*?"

She met his gaze, and grinned. "Remarkably so. There, all done. I'll give the wounds a quick wipe with the cloth – it'll sting a little – and then you can rest at last."

Gideon gave a sigh of relief, sitting up gingerly. She saw how stiffly he moved, and how goosebumps broke out over his skin.

"You should sleep down here tonight," Prudy said abruptly. "Until Joseph and Agatha can help you get upstairs. It's warm and light here, and if I bring blankets and pillows, you'll be comfortable enough on the chaise longue. What do you say?"

He shot a quick, surprised glance at her.

"But this is your parlour, Prudy."

She shrugged. "I won't be using it overnight. Your room is dark and cold, and I think you'll dry off better here. I'll bring a fresh change of clothes – and don't worry, I won't outrage your maiden bashfulness by helping you change – and you can sleep here. What do you say?"

He chewed his lip for a long moment, then nodded, almost reluctantly.

"Very well. And... and thank you, Prudy. You've done a great deal for me tonight."

She bit back a smile of triumph.

"Well, I am an *excellent* wife," she acknowledged, gathering together the bowl of bloody water and various cloths and so on. "I will be back soon with supplies. For now, you should rest."

She'd expected more resistance, but by the time Prudy returned with blankets and pillows, Gideon was lying down on the chaise longue, already asleep. She gingerly laid the blankets over him and propped a pillow under his head, then stole away, careful not to wake him.

Chapter Thirteen

The tight pain which flared across Gideon's shoulder whenever he moved had begun to dissipate lately. For that, he was grateful. He might have endured much worse pain for much longer, but that didn't mean he was willing to endure it again in a smaller dose.

The bullet wound was healing nicely. Gideon knew he'd been lucky, even if Agatha hadn't kept repeating how lucky he'd been, with an almost reproachful expression on her face as if he wasn't appreciating it enough.

He felt sorry for her – she'd likely never take time off to visit her family again, terrified that Gideon would get himself into some scrape or other. That wasn't fair on her, not one bit.

That had been the way of things for a good long while now. Gideon weighed down whoever was foolish enough to stay around him. Agatha and Joseph, and no doubt his poor wife would follow soon enough.

I think it would be a great relief to everybody, he thought bad-temperedly, *if I could just do the decent thing and die.*

He'd thought that more than once, but refrained from saying it. People tended to get upset. Last time he made a similar comment, his Uncle Bartholomew had very nearly forced him to move into the city so that they could share apartments.

Now *that* would have been a disaster.

"Are you warm enough, my lord?" Agatha asked, poised with a scarf in case Gideon should complain of a chill. Joseph loitered anxiously in the background, carrying a pair of garden shears in lieu of doing actual work.

Gideon's cheeks burned. Had there ever been a time he hadn't been so reliant on other? Had he ever been anything other than a burden?

"I'm fine, thank you, Agatha."

"Now, are you sure? Are your stitches pulling? Cool weather can make the skin tighten, you know."

Gideon said nothing. He did know, but Prudy had done a remarkably good job of stitching up his skin. Agatha thought differently, but that was neither here nor there.

Prudy herself had gone for a walk. She'd taken herself on a great many walks in the previous week and a half, while Gideon lay in his darkened bedroom, gradually summoning the strength to take himself to his study, and then out into the gardens to build up his strength again. He had wondered, more than once, how his little wife chose to entertain herself.

She'd come to visit him, and that had been a shock. Agatha had made valiant efforts to keep her away, claiming that Gideon needed his rest, needed quiet, needed peace.

He wasn't sure whether to be disappointed or thrilled that Prudy had persevered, pushing past the formidable guardian with treats, cups of tea, and the occasional novel.

Their conversations had been short and shallow, but they were conversations all the same. Now he had a little stack of novels and poetry books piled beside his bed, none of which he intended to read.

It was Prudy, in fact, who'd gone into the forest in the days after the accident, when Gideon was still collapsed in bed, and found his walking-stick. Gideon was glad. It had been a present from his uncle, the first step towards self-sufficiency, and it meant a great deal to him. He was leaning on it now, wondering whether his latest attempt at saying *thank-you* to his wife would be noticed.

The answer came sooner than expected.

Prudy herself appeared at the other end of the long gravel walk which half-circled the house, the only stretch of the gardens Agatha would let him walk upon. She was wearing a deeply unfashionable blue organdie gown, rather loose-fitting but undeniably comfortable. Gideon thought it suited her.

The voluminous skirts billowed around Prudy's legs as she spotted them and began to run. Towards them. He flinched, entertaining a brief fantasy where his legs were as strong as they had once been, allowing him to turn tail and run back into the house.

They weren't, so Gideon had to stand where he was, arm looped through Agatha's, and wait for Prudy's arrival. Arrive she did, in a shower of gravel.

"Good gracious," Agatha said, which seemed to cover everything.

"Is he for me?" Prudy gasped, breathless. "Oh, Gideon, do

say that he is. He is *beautiful."*

Agatha glanced between them, bewildered. "I don't understand, my lord. What's going on?"

"It seems," Gideon said slowly, "That my wife has discovered her present. Joseph must have brought it in this morning."

"Indeed I did, my lord," Joseph said, shuffling up at just the right moment. "The finest little thing you ever did see. Small for a stallion, but dapper, and high stepping. Silver, he is, with a red mane and tail and a red strawberry on his forehead. Very unusual, and most beautiful. Good breeding, too."

Prudy made a brief, dismissive gesture. "Breeding hardly matters, but he *is* beautiful. And I'm going to call him just that – Strawberry. It's a fine name, don't you think?"

Gideon wrinkled his nose, just managing to smooth the expression away before she noticed.

Or so he thought. Prudy narrowed her gaze at him.

"Oh, do you not approve, my dearest husband? I suppose you'd rather I call him Socrates, or Pythagoras."

"I think that Pythagoras is a fine name for a horse."

"So is Strawberry," she responded, holding her ground.

Gideon gracefully inclined his head, admitting defeat. "So it is, so it is. Strawberry is an excellent name. I'm sure it suits him very well."

Prudy deflated, just a little. She was eyeing him strangely, and Gideon forced himself to meet her gaze.

That odd fluttering was back in his chest again. He'd put it down to any number of things in the earlier days of their acquaintanceship, but it was getting harder and harder to think of rational, boring explanations as to why his heart was doing somersaults under his ribs whenever Prudy entered the room.

He tried telling himself that it was because she had saved his life, and was richly deserving of a little adulation, but that explanation barely registered as half-sensible.

Prudy looked beautiful today, in a blowsy, uncoordinated sort of way. Not that Gideon intended to risk offering a compliment. He would almost certainly end up insulting the poor girl.

Her hair was gathered and pinned into a disheveled bun, which seemed practical if not fashionable, and strands were escaping to sit on her neck. There was a smudge on her cheek, the origins of which Gideon did not care to think too hard about, and something that looked suspiciously like a root vegetable stuck out of her pocket. She was wearing a loose linen shirt under her organdie gown, the sleeves billowing over her hands, the collar poking up around her neck, in great need of pressing.

She looked like a careless country maiden, a woman with far too much on her mind to care about tweaking her hair or hanging gold earrings in her ears.

A woman with purpose. A happy woman.

She glanced up at him, in the middle of listing Strawberry's many perfections, and smiled widely.

The smile was a surprise. That is, the smile directed at *him*, full and guileless and beaming, was a surprise. Gideon sucked in a breath, and his heart pounded giddily once again.

"I can't wait to show Cynthia," Prudy was saying. "Not that she knows anything about horses, but she does like pretty ones. And once I'm comfortable riding him, we might even..." she trailed off, faltering, and glanced up at Gideon again. Her expression had changed now, with some of that happiness fading away.

"Ah. Never mind."

Gideon realized with a rush that she was thinking of inviting more people over, perhaps a riding outing. She was the sort of woman with a lot of friends, he knew that much.

Joseph was there, fortunately oblivious to the sudden tension in the air. He shuffled closer, asking Prudy some question or other about the upkeep of her new horse. With her attention distracted, Gideon glanced around, wondering if he could set off for the house before she remembered him.

Agatha's hand closed around his wrist.

"It would be a nice thank-you," she said, voice barely louder than a whisper.

It was, of course, far overstepping the mark for a housekeeper to say such a thing. Agatha, however, was not the sort of woman who acknowledged or even noticed *marks*.

Gideon sighed. "You're right, of course."

He waited for Prudy to glance his way, eventually clearing his throat for attention.

"I thought perhaps you might like to throw a party here,"

111

Gideon said. There was a brief silence after he spoke, when everybody, including himself, reeled at the words which had exited his mouth. Prudy looked baffled. Joseph looked incredulous. Agatha, to her credit, looked rather smug.

"A party?" Prudy managed. "But I thought you didn't... that is to say, you never..."

She trailed off, and Agatha immediately took the hint, looking Joseph and towed him away. Their footsteps crunched off into the distance, leaving Gideon and Prudy alone.

He felt suddenly shy, like a boy trying to talk to a new friend. His shoulder throbbed, and his leg hurt too, a familiar aching pain that was nonetheless difficult to manage. He leaned a little harder on his cane, the tip sinking deep into the gravel and making him tip drunkenly to one side.

"I didn't mean to make you uncomfortable," Prudy said quietly. "I wasn't trying to hint at... what I mean, I think, is that I know you don't particularly want to have visitors here. You weren't comfortable with Cynthia, and I ought to have taken that into consideration. The horse is beautiful. I'm grateful, and it was very thoughtful of you. I'm quite content. The truth is..." she trailed off, shifting from foot to foot. "The truth is that I can be a little selfish at times."

"I think all of us can."

"No, I mean that I can be thoughtless. I can be a little too interested in gossip and entirely too wrapped up in myself. It's rather shocking, I must say." She gave a nervous little giggle. "But I don't expect to have my way here. I suppose I'm maturing, don't you think?"

Gideon bit the inside of his cheek. "That's kind of you to say. I haven't been particularly friendly to you, have I?"

"No," she conceded. "You have not."

"I didn't wish to be married. I know you didn't, either. I've been childish. The very least I can do is to let you have a party, for heaven's sake."

Prudy blinked at him. Perhaps she kept expecting him to take it back.

"Well, if you're sure," she said at last. "We could invite your friend, Patrick Devin."

Gideon flinched. It had been so long since he'd spoken to

Patrick. Would he really find himself face to face with his old friend, here at the wreck of his home?

He met Prudy's eye. She was watching him anxiously.

"We don't have to invite him if it's not necessary, but it would look odd, especially when all the other locals are coming."

Gideon swallowed. "The… the locals are coming? I rather thought it would just be your friends."

"Well, of course I'll invite my friends – Cynthia and her family, and Blanche, if she'll come, and… I thought it would be nice to invite the locals. They'll be my neighbours, and they were so helpful when my carriage broke down. I thought it would be nice."

Gideon rallied. "It will be nice. Well, I suppose… I suppose I can let you get on with it, can't I? Invitations, and talking to Agatha about food and so on…can you manage that?"

"Oh, absolutely," Prudy said, beaming. The smile sent a flutter into Gideon's chest again. He swallowed hard, trying to get the feeling to go away. It would not.

Her gaze was already inward-looking, thinking about the party to come, about the RSVPs, the finger food, and whatever else was included in a party. He had a feeling that this one was going to be big. Already he could feel his stomach tightening, tension spreading throughout his frame at the thought of what was to come.

There would be no escape. He would have to *socialize*.

***

"Well done, your lordship," Agatha said later, escorting him back to the house. The clouds had covered the sun, and it was getting cold. Gideon was getting to the end of his strength and was already thinking of the comfortable desk chair in his study.

"I do wonder what I've unleashed," Gideon mumbled. "You were right, though. I'm glad I did it. Prudy deserves a party."

"She seems to enjoy the organizing of it almost as much as the prospect of the party itself," Agatha chuckled, shaking her head. "I've already got a list as long as my arm for what to cook, bless her. She's excited."

Gideon bit back a smile. He couldn't deny that it had felt good, seeing Prudy so excited, looking forward so intensely to the

113

party. It almost drowned out the dread in the pit of his stomach.

"It'll do you good, too," Agatha added, and Gideon flinched.

"I beg your pardon?"

"You heard me, your lordship. It'll do you good to see some people. Show the locals you aren't a monster who eats children in the night."

"Or eats animals raw, leaving their bodies scattered all over the forest?"

Agatha pursed her lips. She didn't much approve of *that* particular rumour.

"Exactly so. And maybe you'll make some friends, if you aren't as stiff as you usually are."

"I don't have a great deal of control over my joints, Agatha."

"You know fine well it's not your joints we're talking of, my lord."

"Hmph. Well, I'll have to talk to people, won't I? But nobody will be interested in me, you mark my words. It'll all be Prudy they're here to see. She's the one who will charm them. She'll be the one everybody wants to talk to."

Agatha shot him a narrow look. "Don't be so sure about that, my lord."

Chapter Fourteen

Rycroft Hall, was as it turned out, cleaned up very nicely. Prudy had overheard at least half a dozen people exclaiming at the timeless beauty of the place, at the vaulted ceilings and highly polished floors. Every time, Prudy smiled to herself and glided past, pretending not to notice.

Cynthia and her family were here, of course. As if they'd miss such a talked-about event. There hadn't been a single invitation turned down, and Agatha reported the town was buzzing with it. The mysterious, macabre Rycroft Hall throwing open its doors for a gathering? Unheard of. Nobody wanted to miss it.

Prudy moved past another group of people, a few locals whose names she'd taken the trouble to memorize earlier, and smiled and waved at them, laughing at a few more compliments on her gown.

Where was Gideon?

More importantly, why did it matter so intensely to Prudy where Gideon was? He hadn't been in the thick of the conversation earlier, but that was no surprise.

She saw him after a few moments' searching, huddled in a corner. Patrick Devin stood beside Gideon, and beside *him* was a tall, brown-haired woman with an easy smile and a hooked nose.

Gideon met her eye, and a look of relief swept over his face, so intense that Prudy stopped short. She moved over without being beckoned and smiled up at the guests.

"It's a pleasure, Lady Rycroft," Patrick said, bowing over her hand. "I've often wondered how well you settled in after I left you. How are you?"

"Very well, thank you," Prudy responded, the response rising automatically to her lips.

"This is my wife, Mrs Jane Devin. Jane, this is Lady Prudence Rycroft."

Bows and pleasantries were exchanged.

"I confess, this is the first time I've ever been inside Rycroft Hall," Jane said, smiling. She had an easy, open way about her that tended to put people at ease. Prudy liked her already, and Gideon seemed – if not comfortable, certainly more comfortable than he might have been otherwise.

"Would you like a tour?" Prudy found herself offering. "Before we sit down to supper, at least?"

"I should like that very much. I should warn you, a storm is brewing, and some guests may choose to leave early this evening," Jane added, linking her arm through Prudy's.

Prudy managed to suppress a shudder. Just her luck, all these storms.

"Your party is beautiful, by the way," Jane remarked, after a few moments' wandering in the hall. "Everybody is having a good time. You're an excellent hostess."

"Everybody is having a good time?" Prudy asked archly. "Even Gideon?"

She immediately wished she'd been a little more discreet. Jane, however, did not flinch.

"He is comfortable with Patrick," she responded easily. "I haven't met him often, but Patrick talks about him a great deal. They were close friends, once."

"Not so much anymore, I've heard," Prudy said, before she could stop herself. "It's a pity."

"It is a pity. Patrick misses his friend. You should have seen how thrilled he was when the invitation arrived. I know it's none of my business, but I'd like to see Rycroft Hall open more often these days."

Prudy bit her lip. "I'd like that, too."

"Baby steps, of course," Jane said, as if they were discussing nothing heavier than the weather.

Perhaps that was a poor choice of words. The weather, at that moment, was grey and ominous, with rain lashing the windows. Prudy shuddered, suddenly feeling keen on getting back to the warm, brightly lit ballroom.

As if she sensed her feelings, Jane's arm tightened around Prudy's.

"It'll be fine, you know," she said quietly. "You're exactly what he needs. That's what Patrick kept saying, that first night he met you. I've been dying to meet you for such a long time."

Before Prudy could ask what that meant, their circuit brought them round into the Great Hall, and the noise and laughter washed over them. Prudy spotted Gideon in the same

116

corner as before, smiling at something Patrick had said. A feeling of contentment rushed over her, nothing she'd quite ever felt before. She wanted nothing more than to avoid the knots of young people her age, all wanting to chat and gossip, and find Gideon right away.

And then a familiar face appeared in front of her.

"Miss Copperwell!" Isaac Bates beamed. "In the flesh! It's wonderful to see you."

"Mr. Bates," Prudy managed, a little stupefied. "I... I didn't expect to see you here."

That was a rather polite way of saying *you were not invited.*

Isaac didn't seem upset. "I know I didn't receive a personal invite," he acknowledged, "But I was in the area, and thought I might visit. I hope you aren't upset?"

"No, no, of course not," Prudy said, recovering. "It's Lady Rycroft now, by the way."

Isaac's smile tightened. "Yes, your marriage came as a surprise. I suppose congratulations are in order."

She noticed that he didn't actually offer congratulations but smiled as if he had.

"Well, you are welcome, of course, Mr. Bates. Do excuse me."

She and Jane stepped past the man, and carried on towards their husbands.

"He seemed a little too eager to speak to you," Jane remarked.

"Oh, I think Mr. Bates wanted to marry me. We would never have suited."

Jane pursed her lips. "Do you think he knows that?"

Before Prudy could respond, they had reached Gideon's corner, and found that a knot of guests had gathered around. Poor Gideon looked a little panicked.

"I am just saying, Mr. Bout," Gideon said, his voice a trifle too loud for polite company, "If you had mended your fences when you were asked, the pigs would never have gotten in. Besides, is this not a problem for the magistrate?"

Mr. Bout, an already red-faced farmer, was getting redder and redder by the minute, swelling up like an outraged partridge.

"Well, the last earl of Rycroft *always* managed these things," the man blustered, glancing around at his friends for support. They nodded encouragingly. All of them, to Prudy's untrained eye, looked like farmers.

"This earl will not," Gideon snapped back, in a tone entirely too sharp for a polite gathering such as this. "If you can bring each petty squabble and quarrel to an earl, who is *not* a justice and who has *no* authority or training beyond his own title, what sort of decisions will be given out?"

"We've always trusted the earl in the past."

Gideon leaned forward, resting heavily on his cane. "And *why*? The magistrate is authorized to dispense justice."

"Well, the earl..."

"The magistrate, Mr. Foulkes, is right here. Why not take this matter to him?"

Consternation spread over Mr. Bout's face. Prudy could guess what was going on here. If the magistrate was involved, there would be procedures to follow, questions that must be asked, investigations that must be concluded to the satisfaction of all involved.

Asking the earl, however, involved none of this nonsense, and if they did not receive an answer they liked, they could always go to the magistrate after all.

They could also complain, if the earl gave them an answer they disliked. It was a trap that Gideon clearly did not intend to fall into.

On the other hand, Prudy could see the farmers getting more and more annoyed, outraged at Gideon's sharp, dismissive tone.

This was how malicious gossip turned into rumour, and rumour rapidly turned into fact and folklore. It was how the stories of a monster at Rycroft Hall might become a little more man-shaped.

Clearing her throat, Prudy stepped forward, smiling.

"Gentlemen, good evening! Are you enjoying the claret? My dear Gideon insisted on bringing up the best stuff from our cellars," she said smoothly, sliding her arm through Gideon's. He shot her a quick, baffled look, but mercifully fell silent.

"It is good stuff," Mr. Bout muttered, taking another mouthful.

"I hear that the well was recently repaired, is that so?"

"The path to the well," somebody else spoke up. "It is paved, now. It'll make it a little less slippery and muddy in bad weather."

Prudy squeezed Gideon's arm, shooting a calculatedly doting look up at him.

"Oh, my Gideon is so thoughtful. You should see him up in his study, thinking of what else he can do to benefit the people of Dalton Town. I was quite shocked to hear that there is *no punishment* for collecting deer and rabbits for one's family on Rycroft land! I'm sure you can imagine how unusual that is. I know some lords and barons back in Derby who would dearly love to slice off poacher's hands for simply taking a rabbit. Silly, is it not? Gideon is far too kind for such a thing."

There were shuffling feet at this, and a few embarrassed affirmations. Prudy was careful to keep her face easy and open, as if she had no idea what she was doing.

The trouble with people seemed to be that they quickly forgot the good things they'd received. It was easily done. When somebody did a favour so regularly, people began to think that it was their due. They stopped seeing it as a favour, but simply something that *happened*.

It did not hurt to remind them, every now and then, as Prudy was doing.

"I don't believe I congratulated you on your marriage, Lord Rycroft," Mr. Bout said suddenly, clearing his throat and changing the subject. "Lady Rycroft is a fine, beautiful young woman. You are a lucky man indeed."

"I am," Gideon mumbled, looking like a cornered rabbit.

"Oh, *I* am the lucky one," Prudy cooed, tightening her grip. "Am I not, dearest?"

Gideon blinked at her. "Uh, I believe so."

She chuckled as if he'd made a tremendous joke.

The knot of people began to break up a little after that, and soon enough it was only the four of them again. Jane and Patrick's arms were interlinked, and they looked highly amused. It struck Prudy that even though they were not evenly matched in looks – Patrick was a remarkably handsome man, but Jane was rather plain – she had seldom seen a pair so much in love.

"I think she's far too clever for you, Gideon," Patrick remarked, smiling.

Gideon sighed heavily. "This is not news to me, Patrick."

They were still laughing when the first thunderclap rolled through the room, making a few people exclaim. Almost without thinking, Prudy tightened her grip on Gideon's arm.

Chapter Fifteen

The last guests had gone, and Gideon could finally allow himself to breathe.

The party hadn't been the horror-filled evening he'd expected. Mostly, Gideon had stuck with Patrick and his wife, Jane. She was a pleasant woman, and he felt guilty for not meeting her earlier.

Not a word of reproach had crossed Patrick's lips, though. No *why did you never come to call,* or *why haven't you answered my letters?* He'd only shook Gideon's hand, smiled, and nudged his shoulder like they used to do when they were boys.

"Good to see you, old friend," Patrick had said. Cool and simple, as if no time had passed.

They'd talked about everything and nothing, and the time had swum past. Of course, there'd been people who demanded his attention. Conversations that had to be had, but once he got going, it wasn't so terrible after all.

The candlelight did a good job of hiding the pockmarks on Gideon's skin, and so did his high collar and well-tied cravat wrapped securely around his neck.

All in all, the night was manageable. In fact, Gideon thought that if Prudy wanted to host another such night, he might not object to allowing it, if Patrick and Jane might be invited.

He eased himself down the last flight of stone stairs and staggered into the kitchen.

It had been chaos earlier, with the two maids plus Agatha's niece toiling in the kitchen. Joseph's nephew had been trussed up into something that looked like livery and had gone through the party with trays of drinks and food. There'd been no spillages, no major accidents, and Gideon thought that he'd been particularly charming.

It was just Agatha in there now, tired and sweaty, wiping down the counters. She glanced up at Gideon and smiled.

"Did you enjoy the evening, your lordship?"

"Enjoy is a strong word," Gideon remarked, leaning heavily against the doorway. His leg was aching, his palm sore from gripping the top of his cane too tightly, and on cue, his shoulder had begun to throb dully. "The food was a great success, Agatha. Thank you. You did remarkably well to pull it all together in so short a time. Your family also did well. I'll add a bonus onto their agreed wages."

"They were happy to help," Agatha said firmly. "In my opinion, opening up Rycroft Hall in this way is the best thing for everybody involved. It'll show the people that there's no *monster* here, that it's all superstition and rumour, and that you and your Lady Rycroft are wonderful people."

Lady Rycroft. His Lady Rycroft. The name still felt odd, as if it belonged to somebody else, and a lady... well, that was too odd for Gideon to get his head around at all.

She won't be here long, he reminded himself. *A few parties, until the novelty wears off, and then Prudy will be off home to Derby.*

What will I do then?

He ignored that thought. "Where is Lady Rycroft, Agatha?"

"Gone up to her room, I think. Exhausted, she is."

Outside, the rain intensified, rattling angrily against the windowpanes as if it were trying to come in.

The weather had set in earlier in the evening, grey skies turning darker still and the rain starting to squeeze out. The wind raked through the trees outside, their dark shapes dancing in the forest. Every now and then a rumble of thunder rolled through the air in the wake of sky-splitting lightning. It would be breathtaking to watch, but Gideon had learned his lesson about going wandering during storms.

"It was nice to see Mr. Devin here again," Agatha said suddenly, with calculated casualness. "Word in town had it that he was looking forward to this evening very much."

Gideon bit his lip. "I was glad to see Patrick. I've missed his friendship."

Agatha put down the wet rag she'd been using to wipe down the counter and looked Gideon full in the eyes.

"A man can't go through life friendless," she said shortly. "And friendship, like everything else, must be worked at."

Gideon sighed, shuffling around to make the long climb back up the stairs to the Great Hall.

"You know, some masters would take exception to you

122

speaking like that, Agatha."

"I daresay they would. Are you taking exception?"

He smiled wryly over his shoulder. "No, I'm not. Goodnight, Agatha."

Upstairs, the candles flickered weakly in their sconces. Gideon couldn't have said when the stores of good wax candles had appeared, lit and cheerful along the hallways and in the corners of the Great Hall, but it was definitely after Prudy's arrival.

He should have complained about the wastefulness, but it *was* nice to have light. It made the place seem warmer, somehow. Warmer and more like a home.

It occurred to him that Rycroft Hall, while it had been many things, never seemed to be a *home*.

Was that what it was now? Home, after all these years?

Swallowing hard, Gideon slowed outside of Prudy's room. He noticed briefly that the corridor was a little less well-swept than the rest of the hall. Why were there footprints in the dust, then, leading along past Prudy's room? Did she go wandering in the dark?

He was imagining things. Already, Gideon could have sworn he saw a shape move in the Great Hall, but of course there was nobody here but the four of them – Agatha and Joseph downstairs, and he and Prudy upstairs. One's mind could play tricks on you, when the light was gloomy enough.

The candles flickered, and the image disappeared, and Gideon assumed he must have imagined it. Clearing his throat and smoothing out his waistcoat, he reached out and rapped at the door.

He waited, but there was no answer. Frowning, Gideon knocked again. She must be awake, as there was a beam of light coming out from under the door.

When there was still no answer, he sucked in a breath and tentatively turned the handle, ready to slam the door shut should he spot steam coming out from the washroom, or glimpse Prudy getting changed for bed.

Instead, the room was just... just empty.

The heavy velvet curtains were open, left as they'd been flung open that morning. The bed was turned down for sleep, and he spotted Prudy's ballgown draped carefully over the dressing-table seat.

But where was *she*?

"Prudy?" Gideon called tentatively, taking a step into the room. "Are you well?"

On cue, a tremendous slash of lightning split the sky, and a roll of thunder shook the room right after. Even Gideon, who found storms soothing in an odd sort of way, winced and squinted against the blaze of light.

The afterglow of the lightning faded away, although the bolt of light reappeared whenever he closed his lids. The buttery light of the candle seemed pale in comparison.

The room was most certainly empty.

"Prudy?" he tried again.

When the door to the large wardrobe creaked open just a little, he nearly jumped out of his skin.

"*Prudy*? Why are you in the wardrobe?" he managed at last, shuffling closer.

He was sure his eyes had deceived him, but no, there was Prudy, in her nightdress and a robe, huddled sheepishly inside the wardrobe itself.

"I just... I just wanted a little peace and quiet," she managed lamely.

He blinked. "Peace and quiet? What..."

The answer to his unspoken question came almost at once. Lightning lit up the room, and thunder rolled. Gideon flinched, but Prudy gave a squeak of panic, retreating further into the wardrobe, clothes flopping around her head and hiding her expression.

In the quiet that followed, Gideon was shocked to hear his wife breathing shallowly, almost in panic.

"I don't like storms," she said, after a long pause. "I haven't liked them ever since I was a child. They don't seem so bad in the city, but out here, in the middle of nowhere, with everything so *dark*..." she broke off with a shudder.

Gideon bit his lip. "I see."

"I'll be fine. You can go to bed, if you like. I'm sure it'll ease off eventually."

Gideon said nothing. Somebody had casually mentioned that the storm was set to last into the early hours of the morning, in which case Prudy might find herself spending the whole night in

124

the wardrobe.

"Wouldn't you feel more comfortable in the bed?" he asked, and then immediately wished he hadn't.

Prudy didn't seem to take offence.

"No, I like small spaces."

"I see."

He seemed to be claiming that he *saw* a great deal lately, but none of it was true. Shifting from foot to foot, Gideon finally made a decision. He hobbled towards the wardrobe, and Prudy peered warily out at him.

"I'm not coming out," she said at last. "You can try and drag me out if you want, but I'll just kick your bad leg out from under you."

"How delightful. I'm not in the habit of dragging people anywhere. I'm not here to pull you out of the wardrobe. However, I would be obliged if you'd move over."

Baffled, Prudy did just that, and Gideon slowly and painfully lowered himself into the wardrobe beside her.

It was not, by any stretch of the imagination, comfortable. Wardrobes were not designed for sitting in, after all.

It was all hard, unyielding wood, and fabric hanging from above tickled his face and neck. He was obliged to frequently brush a lacy hem out of his eyes, as it seemed determined to rest over the top of his head.

Now that he was *inside* the wardrobe, he could see that Prudy had brought a few pillows and cushions in there, and a blanket to drape around herself. Sensible, really. There wasn't room in the wardrobe for much else.

"What are you doing?" Prudy asked, recovering herself.

He arched an eyebrow. "Why don't you take a guess as to what I'm doing?"

She sighed. "I don't need pity."

"I'm not offering it. I must say, though, this is an extreme reaction. A great many people don't enjoy storms, but not everybody goes crawling into a wardrobe at the first whisper of thunder."

She fell silent for a long time before responding.

"When I was eight, I went out for a walk in the woods," she said at last. "Mama said not to go far, because it was going to rain, but I fancied myself as quite the little adventurer, and I wasn't in the least bit afraid of rain. I went by myself, which I wasn't meant to do. I should have brought my sister, Catherine, but she was reading a book and I was at the age when I thought I could do everything myself, and rather resented being watched over."

"I recall that age," Gideon said dryly, to reassure her that he was listening more than anything else. She shifted, bringing them a little closer together. Their shoulders were pressing together now, as there was really not enough room for two people to sit in that wardrobe. Gideon was reminded once again that wardrobes were really *not* for sitting in.

"So off I went," Prudy continued, gaze distant. "I reached the top of a hill, which was my goal, and that was when the rain started. A storm set in."

She shuddered a little, squeezing her eyes closed.

"I'll never forget it. The storm was right overhead. Lightning seemed to set the sky on fire, and the thunder was deafening. I've never experienced a storm like it. Afterwards, there was all kinds of damage done to the surrounding area, and people do still talk about that storm. Most people were sensible enough to huddle in their houses and wait for it to pass, but I was out in the open, with only a large oak tree on top of a hill for shelter. It was terrifying. I was never so frightened in my life. I remember pressing my hands over my ears and closing my eyes, and telling myself that the storm couldn't last forever and that it would pass soon, and I would be quite alright. You think that, at that age. That whatever happens, you'll be *quite alright*. Well, it's not true."

"Were you hurt?"

She shook her head. "No, but I could have easily died. Lightning struck the tree. I didn't know then not to shelter under a tree during a storm. Branches fell, and the whole thing split open, burning in an instant. I can still smell burning and scorched wood. The smell of wood fires made me feel ill for years afterwards. My ears were ringing, the hem of my dress burned, and I don't know how I escaped not being hit by the lightning. I ran down the hill, lightning and thunder all around me. And then, at the bottom, I saw a little shack."

"A house?"

"No, just a shed, a storage shed. I yanked open the door –

mercifully, it was not locked – and threw myself inside. It was full of things – gardening implements, plant pots, that sort of thing. The thunder was still loud, but muffled. I know now that I could still have been struck by lightning, but at the time, it just... it just felt safe. I stayed there for hours, until the storm passed." She paused, shrugging. "Then I went home, and got scolded for getting so wet and muddy."

He sucked in a breath. "You didn't tell them?"

"Not for a while. Mama and Papa would only have been angry that I took such a risk. I told Catherine eventually, and one or two friends. You see, I can still see the lightning when I close my eyes. It terrifies me. Every time I hear thunder and see the sky light up, I'm back on the tree, watching lightning arc down that poor old oak tree. I know it's silly, but I feel as though I *cursed* that tree."

"It's likely that the tree was the highest point around," Gideon commented. "And so the lightning would naturally..."

She gave him a look. "Yes, I know that, thank you very much. As I say, I know I'm a silly fool, but..."

"You're not a silly fool," Gideon said sharply. "Some people are terrified of mice or spiders, and those creatures are much less harmful than *lightning*. Storms are more dangerous than people know. It's rational to be afraid of them."

"Yes, but it's not rational to crawl into wardrobes to escape from them."

"No," he conceded, "But you'll never learn to get over your fear by telling yourself you are a fool and ought to be ashamed. In my experience, changing anything about oneself has to come from a place of positivity. If you don't like yourself, you won't have the motivation to change yourself."

She lifted an eyebrow. "Well, I didn't say that I didn't like myself."

He flushed. "I apologise. I always say the wrong thing, truly."

To his shock – and possibly hers – Prudy reached out, taking his hand. His skin was warm and soft, fingers long and curled around his.

"You don't say the wrong thing," she said firmly. "I... I'm glad you're here, Gideon. I didn't expect you to sit here in a wardrobe with me tonight."

Another roll of thunder rumbled outside, and Prudy's hand

127

tightened around his.

A lump had risen to Gideon's throat, and he found himself watching Prudy's face, half-shadowed and turned away to look out of the window.

"I don't mind," he said at last. "It's quite comfortable here, once you get used to it."

Chapter Sixteen

Prudy woke first.

The first thing she noticed was that her neck hurt, and her legs had gone to sleep.

Well, that was simply to be expected when one spent the night in a wardrobe. It wouldn't be the first time she crawled into a tight little space during a storm, and she reckoned it would not be the last. Places that reminded her of that godsend little shack always evened out her feelings enough to endure the rattling thunder and painful lightning.

The second thing she noticed was that she was curled up around another person, her head on their chest.

It was Gideon, of course. Memories from last night came crowding in. Gideon, shuffling into the room, a look of determination on his face when he lowered himself into the wardrobe. Gideon, talking in a low voice as the candle burned low. Gideon's arm around her shoulder.

He still had his arm around her shoulder, the warm weight of it reassuring and *grounding*, somehow.

She had slumped over towards him during the night – they'd fallen asleep at some point, although Prudy could not have said when – and her head rested on his shoulder. Her ear was against his chest, and if she held her breath, she could hear the regular *thump-thump* of his heart.

Gingerly, so as not to disturb him, Prudy sat up. The hems of her dresses, hanging above their heads, tickled her cheeks.

Poor Gideon did not fit in the wardrobe at all. His legs stuck out comically across the floor, walking-stick discarded at his side. His head slumped to one side, forehead resting against the wooden inside of the wardrobe, and she was willing to bet he'd have marks on his skin when he woke up.

It was, of course, morning. The light filtering in was golden and pure, no hint of last night's storm to be seen.

Wincing at the pain, Prudy straightened her cramped limbs until she could manoeuvre herself into a half-standing position, and hobbled over to the window.

Outside, the gardens looked fresh. Washed clean, almost.

She eased open the window, and the delightful smell of wet earth and fresh grass rolled in, along with birdsong and the scent of sunshine, if sunshine could be said to have a smell.

Prudy thought, in the strangest way, that it did.

She heard rustling behind her and glanced over her shoulder.

"What time is it?" Gideon murmured groggily, rubbing his eye with one knuckle. His black hair was disarranged, his cravat tugged loose to reveal those silvery pockmarks leading down towards his chest. He looked younger than ever, more like a sleepy, dishevelled young man than a serious Gothic villain.

A wave of affection swept over Prudy, so intense she nearly staggered backwards. The lump was back in her throat, and her chest tightened almost as badly as it had last night.

"I'm not sure," she managed at last. "Nine or ten, I'd say."

Gideon cursed under his breath. "And yet I still feel as though I haven't slept a wink."

"Well, we did sleep in a wardrobe," Prudy pointed out. "They're not known to allow for good sleep."

"Fair," he acknowledged, reaching for his walking-stick. Gideon began the laborious process of hauling himself to his feet. Prudy itched to help but forced herself to stay back. She'd learned that Gideon liked to be independent and liked to manage himself. Perhaps it was a pride thing, or perhaps he simply knew that relying on others was not a long-term solution, whereas learning to do the thing himself *could be*. So, she stayed where she was, suddenly self-conscious in her nightgown, fingers twisting together in front of her waist.

Gideon pulled himself upright with a grimace and made a pathetic attempt to straighten out his crumpled clothes.

"Why did you come here last night?" Prudy asked, and then immediately regretted it, as it sounded like an accusation.

He sighed. "I came to thank you for arranging such a delightful party. I... well, I won't go so far as to say I *enjoyed* myself, but it was certainly bearable."

She grinned, despite the odd feeling curling in her chest. "Bearable, you say? Well, that is high praise indeed."

"Leave me alone, you wretch. I'm too tired and stiff to think of good words."

"Well, I... I'm glad you came to sit with me. It was pleasant."
Gideon smiled and looked young again.

"It was certainly something new. Do you think... do you think you'd like to take breakfast together?"

"I would love that."

"Excellent. I'll change into fresh clothes."

"I'll see if Agatha can rustle something up for us."

"Agreed."

They parted ways, and Prudy could have sworn she was walking on air.

***

Angry mopping sounds greeted her in the kitchen.

Prudy had quickly thrown on a simple muslin dress, plain and loose-fitting, but perfectly suited to a day spent inside one's home. Frowning, she shuffled further into the kitchen.

"Agatha?"

"In here," came the answer, coming from the scullery.

One of the back doors, leading out into the courtyard where washing was hung up to dry, stood ajar. The floor around the door was wet, and Prudy just had time to glimpse a set of muddy footprints leading away from it, seconds before Agatha's mop squelched over them.

"Sorry about the mess, your ladyship," Agatha said, straightening up from her mopping. "Lord Rycroft must have left the back door open when he came in from his walking about last night, and that's not like him at all. There's mud and water everywhere. Not surprising, with that storm last night, but I found the door ajar when I came up this morning. It's not safe, you know."

Prudy bit the inside of her cheek. "Well, it can't have been Gideon."

"Why not? He often walks around at night, you know that, your ladyship."

Prudy opened her mouth to say that it could *not* have been Gideon, as he'd spent the whole night with her.

Just in time, she bit back the words. Agatha might reach *certain conclusions* if she said that, and Prudy was in no mood to

131

explain her fear of storms and her long-standing habit of riding out particularly bad thunderstorms in wardrobes.

But the footprints could not have been Gideon's, certainly.

"I'll mention it to him," Prudy managed at last. "I came down to ask about breakfast."

"Oh, forgive me, your ladyship! With the late night we all had last night, I didn't think you'd want breakfast until later in the morning, then I was distracted with all this mopping. I'll get something started right away."

"Don't worry about it, Agatha. Could you set the table in the dining room? For us both, please."

Agatha paused, glancing significantly at Prudy. "Eating together, are you?"

Prudy felt her treacherous cheeks begin to heat up. "Yes, we are."

Agatha bit back a smile. "Well, I'm glad to hear that."

Prudy smiled too. The morning suddenly spread out in front of her, bright and happy and full of possibilities. She wanted to sing and maybe dance a little, if Agatha wouldn't think that she was mad.

"Thank you, Agatha! I'll fetch Gideon and we'll be down soon, I'm sure."

"Right you are, your ladyship, right you are."

Your ladyship. For the first time in... well, since *ever*, the title seemed to fit Prudy better than she might have expected.

She all but skipped back up the stairs.

"Gideon?" Prudy called, hurrying along the hallway. "Gideon, Agatha said something about footsteps in..." she pushed open the door without knocking, mind on the wet scullery floor and Agatha's knowing smile, and immediately trailed off.

Gideon stood in the middle of his bedroom, stripped to the waist. He'd changed into a fresh pair of black breeches, and held a white linen shirt in his hands, ready to put on.

He had not, however, put it on.

He had a more defined torso than Prudy might have imagined – *not* that she had imagined it, of course – with the sort of lean muscle a slim man who'd been through the army might be expected to have. His waist was thinner than it should have been, but his arms and chest were still strong, the skin pale as bone.

That was not what immediately caught Prudy's attention. That dubious honour went to the scars.

She could see the spot on his shoulder where the bullet had gone in, the black thread of her own clumsy stitches forming a neat little line. Spiralling away from the bullet wound were the most awful scars Prudy had ever seen.

She had spotted the beginnings of those wounds before, when she'd stitched up his shoulder, and guessed that they only got worse. She was right.

That side of Gideon's chest was thick with scars. What looked like strips of burned skin spiralled around down his arm, almost covering his bicep and thinning out over his forearm. Gouges and pits littered his abdomen, so much so that one side of his waist was knotted and uneven in a way skin ought not to be. What healthy skin he had left was strained to bulging, its natural elastic stretched past its breaking point to compensate for the immovable scar tissue.

"Prudence!" Gideon shouted, and Prudy dragged her gaze up from his ruined chest to meet his eyes.

Gideon was whiter than before – if that was possible – and his lips were pressed together in a thin, angry line. He moved as if to hold up his crumpled shirt in front of his chest, then forced himself to lower his arms again. Almost defiantly.

"Well, well, have a good look, then," he snapped. "You've been nosy about this since you first came here, haven't you? I should have expected this. Barging into my room, not knocking. Go on, take a look. I haven't an inch of healthy skin left on my body; it feels like. Do you want to ask questions? I'm sure you do. Look your fill, ask your questions, then do me the courtesy of leaving me alone."

Prudy recoiled a little from the torrent of anger and words. She almost retreated, scurrying out of the room and slamming the door behind her.

She had no idea what would happen if she did that. Perhaps a rift would open up between them that would not be healed.

She never had to learn, though, because Prudy found herself stepping forward, into Gideon's room, and letting the door swing closed behind her. She folded her arms across her chest.

133

"Stop being so angry," she said shortly. "I should have knocked, of course I should, but it was unintentional. I came up to here to talk to you, not to spy on you. If I was going to spy on you, don't you think I would have done it by now? I am sorry to barge in, it was wrong of me, but I would like to remind you that *you* saw me in the bath once, so I think this makes us even."

Gideon flushed hotly. "Get out."

"You said I could ask questions."

"This is none of your concern."

He began to tug at his shirt, clearly longing to pull it over his head. Prudy noticed for the first time that the scars clustered thickly at Gideon's hip, no doubt plunging down below the waistband to the leg beneath. Coincidentally, Gideon's bad leg.

She bit her lip.

"Does it hurt?"

He paused. "What?"

"The scars. Do they hurt?"

He eyed her for a long minute.

"They did. They're mostly healed now, although the scar tissue generally feels tight at times. I have to apply a lotion to help with that."

Prudy shuffled a little closer. "I can't imagine how agonizing it was when this happened. I... I cut open the back of my shoulder falling from a tree when I was a child, and the pain was awful as it healed. That was just a little gash, no longer than my palm. All of that..." she broke off, shuddering. "I can't imagine how it felt."

Gideon's eyes flickered closed. He swallowed hard, and she traced the movement down the pain column of his throat.

"I thought I would die," he confessed at last. "I *hoped* I would die, because then the pain would stop. I... I remember lying in a stretcher-bed in the army hospital, staring up at the fly-ridden tent ceiling, and praying with all my might to close my eyes and not wake up again. I asked the army chaplain why my prayer wasn't answered, and he simply told me that God wanted me to live, not die, and one day the pain would be an unpleasant memory and no more."

He smiled woodenly and tapped his bad leg. "Perhaps the chaplain hadn't counted on this, eh?"

She swallowed hard. "Gideon, I'm sorry. Did... did you

134

believe that this would make people treat you differently?"

His expression hardened. "My own uncle couldn't look at me when the bandages first came off. Everything changed, Prudy. Everything."

Prudy found that she couldn't find the words to say something. The pain was right there in Gideon's eyes, raw and unrelenting. Not literal pain, but something deeper. She imagined how people like Cynthia and Blanche would recoil if they saw the scars, just as they'd recoiled from his odd style of dress and pockmarked jaw and neck.

On impulse, she reached forward and took Gideon's hand in hers. He dropped the shirt in surprise. His fingers were cool in hers, and Prudy found herself thinking of the way he'd put his arm around her in the wardrobe, angling her so that she rested her head against his shoulder, not on the hard back of the wardrobe itself.

"Can... can you tell me what happened?" she asked at last, voice quiet. "I don't want to pry, believe me. I only want to understand."

He bit his lip, and for a long moment, Prudy wasn't sure whether he was going to yank away his hand and order her out of his room. Perhaps he wasn't sure, either.

"It happened during the war," he said at last, voice hollow. "A cannonball aimed at our store of munitions. We realized too late what they were shooting at. Some men were unluckier than me and were closer to the stores when the explosion happened. I saw a man's head taken clean off by a cannonball. I saw one poor fellow with both legs and an arm blown off, trying to drag himself through the filthy mud. I don't know where he thought he was going, only that he didn't make it to the medical tent. For the best, probably. For my part, I was caught up in the explosion. The surgeons were picking shards of wood and metal out of my body for weeks. I vaguely remember being on fire, I think – this side of my body," he gestured to the side with his bad leg and the thickest scars, "and I was lucky not to lose any limbs. My leg was broken in two places. Cleanish breaks, thankfully, or they'd have cut it off. It was botched, I'm afraid. The leg, that is. There were so many wounded and so few surgeons, it was inevitable. It healed wrongly, and hence the pain and the limp I'll have for the rest of my life. But

I came out of it alive, at the very least."

He shrugged weakly, forcing himself to meet Prudy's gaze.

She drew in a shaky breath. It was like she was there, smelling the bloody sawdust on the floor of the surgeons' rooms, hearing cries for help, tasting the tang of gunpowder on her tongue. She shuddered.

"Oh, Gideon, that's awful. I'm so sorry."

He shrugged. "I was one of the lucky ones."

She moved closer, drawn as if by some kind of magnetism. It was the oddest feeling, almost as if she were being controlled by somebody else. A puppeteer, maybe.

Gideon did not move back, and neither did he drop his gaze from hers. He stood there, one hand in hers, arm limp at his side. Prudy lifted her hand and brushed her questing fingertips across the lumpy skin of his chest.

The scar tissue felt cool under her fingers, thick like a callus, twisted and uneven. It felt *wrong*, but at the same time, his skin had grown around it, and the scars were unmistakeably part of him. There were endless whorls and patterns there, ready to be traced.

She glanced up, and Gideon was still looking at her, face unreadable. Prudy held her breath. Their faces were inches apart, his nose almost touching hers. She could feel Gideon's heart pounding under her palm and knew that hers was beating just as wildly.

He's going to kiss me, Prudy thought vaguely. *Or I'm going to kiss him.*

And then there was a sound on the bell outside, sending a deep, ominous ringing echoing through the house.

Chapter Seventeen

Their guest sat on the sofa opposite in Prudy's parlour, looking extremely displeased and more than a little uncomfortable. She recognized him vaguely from last night – Mr. Foulkes, the magistrate. Cynthia's uncle, actually. Prudy had tried to claim the acquaintance earlier, but the man had brusquely told her that he was here on business, not as a social call.

Prudy judged it best not to mention Cynthia at all, then.

"I'm sure my husband will be down at any minute," she said, for possibly the thousandth time since Agatha had nervously shown the magistrate into the parlour. Had it really only been ten minutes since the bell had rung?

Prudy still felt a little disoriented from *almost* kissing Gideon earlier. Or had he *almost* been about to kiss her? Did it matter? She could almost feel the ridges of his fascinating scars under her fingers.

As soon as the bell had rung, they'd sprang apart, with Gideon yanking his shirt over his head immediately, tucking it safely into his waistband, and that was that. The scars were hidden, and the moment was gone.

And now Prudy was sitting here, feeling out of place in her own parlour, with a grumpy magistrate and two grim-faced young men behind him.

"Would it not be better for me to wait in Lord Rycroft's study, Lady Rycroft?" Mr. Foulkes asked, for the third or fourth time. "No need to concern yourself with this business."

She smiled politely but firmly. At least, so she hoped.

"Here is fine, Mr. Foulkes. My husband is comfortable here. We can discuss business just as easily on sofas as we can on desk chairs, can we not?"

Mr. Foulkes apparently did not believe this at all but was disinclined to correct a lady in her own house. He contented himself with a derisive snort and laced his fingers across his stomach.

More time ticked past, counted painstakingly off on the grandfather clock.

Where are you, Gideon? Prudy thought miserably. *Do hurry up.*

"And you really can't breathe a word of what's going on?" she tried again, although she knew very well what the answer would be.

Mr. Foulkes shot her an unimpressed look. "No, Lady Rycroft. This matter is for Lord Rycroft's ears."

Only, she heard him add mentally.

We'll see about that, you cantankerous old man, she thought sourly.

Just in time, Gideon's footsteps and clacking cane rang out across the Great Hall. Everybody rose to their feet when Gideon came limping in, offering only a brusque apology for his lateness. Prudy didn't rise, being the lady of the house, and it would be a lie if she claimed it didn't make her feel special.

"I'm glad you could join us, Lord Rycroft," Mr. Foulkes said heavily, settling himself down again. "This is a serious and upsetting matter. I recommend we do not bother Lady Rycroft with it."

"It's no bother," Prudy responded sweetly. Gideon did not flinch.

"Lady Rycroft will be staying," he said shortly, in a tone that brooked no refusal. "Now, what is this?"

Mr. Foulkes pursed his lips, snorting in a *be-it-on-your-head* way.

"Very well. Lord Rycroft, a girl has been reported missing on your grounds. Murdered."

***

Things progressed very quickly after that. Gideon fired a number of questions at the magistrate, and received short, informative answers.

The girl's name was Thomasin Wrecker, fourteen years old, and was a child of a local landowner. She had been sent out for water shortly after dawn and had not returned for over an hour. When her mother finally went out to see what had happened, she found her daughter's scarf lying by the path leading to the Rycroft well. The Wrecker family were farmers, not highly born enough to have come to the Rycroft party, but well-known and well-liked in the community.

"I know the family," Gideon responded shortly. His face was whiter than usual, red spots of colour burning on his cheeks. "Why do you believe she is missing?"

"Or taken by somebody," Mr. Foulkes said shortly.

The temperature in the room seemed to drop a few degrees. Prudy shivered, drawing her shawl tighter around herself. She tried not to imagine a young girl of fourteen, staggering along a lonely forest path with a bucket of water in the poor light just after dawn, unaware of the fate which waited for her.

Gideon got unsteadily to his feet. "Take me there."

Mr. Foulkes pursed his lips. "I'm not sure..."

"I must see where she was last seen. As the magistrate, this is your responsibility, but this is my land, and my tenants. Their safety is my responsibility."

"I want to come too," Prudy spoke up. Mr. Foulkes went purple.

"I'm afraid that is not possible, Lady Rycroft."

"Why not?"

"Well, because..."

"I see no reason why Lady Rycroft cannot come," Gideon said shortly, glancing briefly at Prudy. "If her stomach can handle it."

"Lord Rycroft, I must protest in the strongest terms to this idea."

Gideon brushed down his waistcoat. "Your objections are noted. Let's leave at once."

Mr. Foulkes opened and closed his mouth, as if thinking of arguing, but ultimately closed his mouth again, lips pursed tight.

"Very well," he snapped. "If you insist. It's a sorry scene, I must say."

They were a quiet and sombre party going through the woods, which was to be expected en route to a young girl who had gone missing. Prudy thought more than once that it was a mistake to have asked to come, but she felt as though it was the right thing to do. They were *her* tenants, too.

The sound of weeping drifted their way. A cluster of people stood by a little clearing, a tall, ashen-faced man with an arm around a woman of the same age, her face buried in her apron.

She was the one crying.

Gideon limped up to them.

"Mr. and Mrs. Wrecker," he said grimly. "I am at a loss for words! But I can promise that we'll get to the bottom of this."

The woman wept harder, but the man managed a tight nod.

On impulse, Prudy went up to the woman.

"I'm sorry," she whispered. "I'm so sorry."

The woman – Mrs. Wrecker, glanced up from her apron, red-eyed.

"I would usually go to get the water," she whispered. "But I was busy today, so I sent Thomasin. How could I have done that?"

"It wasn't your fault," Prudy reassured her. "You couldn't have known. This is an awful, awful situation. We'll get to the bottom of it."

Mrs. Wrecker sniffed, wiping her nose with the back of her hand. On impulse, Prudy whipped out a handkerchief, and the farmer's wife accepted it with a watery smile.

"My Thomasin was very afraid of the monster, you know," Mrs. Wrecker whispered.

Prudy frowned. "The monster?"

"Aye, the Rycroft Hall monster. The children, they tell stories about it all the time. I thought it was nothing but silliness, but after that..." her face crumpled, chin wobbling, and she buried her face in the handkerchief again. "Maybe she was *right*."

"This whole place is cursed to the rafters," Mr. Wrecker spat, then looked away, flushing, as if he'd just remembered that Lord Gideon Rycroft stood right there, listening. He glanced at the earl, a little shamefaced, then buried his face in his wife's shoulder.

"We must get on, Lord Rycroft," Mr. Foulkes said, a trifle snappily. "The girl must be found soon."

Mrs. Wrecker began to weep silently again at the mention of the missing girl, and Prudy shot Mr. Foulkes a little glare. He didn't appear to have noticed.

"I'll stay here," Prudy said. "I think Mr. and Mrs. Wrecker need a little time to grieve, a little support."

Mr. Foulkes smiled tightly. "I had a feeling, Lady Rycroft, that your sensibilities would get the better of you when it came to finding the missing girl."

Mr. Wrecker's head shot up.

"That missing girl you keep referring to is my daughter," he spat. "My *daughter,* Mr. Foulkes!"

Mr. Foulkes had the decency to blush, reprimanded in front of everybody, but Prudy didn't have the heart to feel smug. A child was missing. She met Gideon's eye, and he gave a brief nod.

"Give them what comfort you can," he said, voice low enough for only Prudy to hear. "Take them back to the Hall and get Agatha to help you. Try and organize some local help for the family and arrange somebody to watch the children. There's no easy way of getting through this for the Wreckers, but at least we can offer some practical help, like rent rebate."

Prudy nodded, and Gideon turned to go.

"Make sure you find who is responsible for this," she said shortly, and turned back to the Wreckers.

***

Gideon's leg was hurting him, probably due to the night he'd spent in the wardrobe, unsurprisingly. He could still feel Prudy's fingers skimming over his chest, the thought lingering. He didn't want it to linger, not now, not with a missing child on his land.

Besides, what was it? Curiosity? He hoped not. Curiosity was nothing more than a passing fancy.

The path they were following had been recently widened and paved, and he knew already that half of the village followed this path to get to the well. Abruptly, the path opened up into a wide clearing, with the well looming in the centre. It was shaded by a neat little roof – Gideon's addition too, as well as the pulley for the bucket.

The bucket lay just beside the well and silently he wished he could see the girl appearing suddenly from the woods. But she did not and he turned away.

"Search the area," he said shortly and a wordless man did just that, scanning the clearing for any signs of the missing girl.

Ignoring the pain in his leg, Gideon limped slowly around the well, taking in every detail.

"No signs of a struggle," he said thoughtfully. "No kicked-up bits of grass, no gouges in the earth. Look, she'd already gotten a pail full of water, and it's not upset."

141

Mr. Foulkes glanced over at the well, where a bucket of water – full to the brim – sat demurely beside the low stone wall, as if it had just been set down for a minute while its carrier summoned up the energy to lift it again.

"She's a small girl," he objected. "How much of a struggle would she have put up?"

"True, but a fourteen-year-old girl can be stronger than people expect. I suspect she was taken by surprise. If she was standing here..." Gideon moved over to the well, angling himself as if he had just set down the pail, "... perhaps she simply wandered off."

They all turned to look.

The forest hemmed in all around the clearing, thick and dark. Silent, too. Gideon knew that silence in a forest was a rare thing. There was generally always *some* noise – leaves rustling or the chirping of insects at the very least. Silence was not, in his experience, normal.

He felt as though he were being watched and rolled his shoulders to rid himself of the feeling.

It didn't work. The discomfort did one thing, at least. It sharpened Gideon's senses, and he realized that something was out of place.

"The undergrowth is trodden down there," he said shortly, pointing with his cane.

"That's fairly ordinary in the forest," Mr. Foulkes said.

Gideon ignored him, limping towards the spot he had pointed out. It did indeed look as though somebody had stumbled through there, but there were no other clues. He'd hoped for a splash of blood, a strand of hair or a piece of fabric caught on a thorn. All there was to see were trodden-down weeds and a scrape on a tree trunk.

Sighing, Gideon backed away. He found Mr. Foulkes behind him.

"The reason I did not want Lady Rycroft with us is because we have something more serious to discuss," he said, voice low enough that only Gideon could hear.

Gideon frowned. "More serious than a missing girl?"

Mr. Foulkes was quiet for a long moment, moving his jaw as if chewing something.

142

"You must know, Lord Rycroft, that you have a reputation as a somewhat strange man," he said at last. "You wander at night – yes, I have heard of that – you isolate yourself, and, until the party recently, nobody in town had ever exchanged a word with you."

A prickle ran down Gideon's spine. "What are you trying to say, then?" he asked sharply. "I feel as though you are accusing me of something."

He was being accused; Gideon realized with a jolt of horror. He was a strange man, an *earl* who ought to be happy and cheerful and social, a man on whose land a girl had just gone missing.

Only a short walk away from his home, in fact. Gideon realised with a bitter jolt that he might as well have asked for help from the men who shot at him as a poacher, since they clearly already knew about his night-time walking habits.

He pressed his lips together and tried to swallow his revulsion.

"Are you saying that I had something to do with Thomasin Wrecker's disappearance?" he said heavily.

Mr. Foulkes looked at him for a long moment, then sighed, shaking his head.

"I'm not saying that, Lord Rycroft. You're an odd man, sure enough – if your lordship will forgive my speaking freely – but I've seen a lot of strange people in my time, and I don't believe you're one of them. Just about everybody in town has visited that well at one time or another, and you've never once crossed their path. I don't believe you had anything to do with this. But you must know that public opinion holds a great deal of sway in a place like this. What I believe may matter very little when compared to what others believe, do you understand?"

Gideon swallowed hard, clenching his teeth. Outrage was pouring up his throat, threatening to spill out over his tongue. How dared they? How *dared* they? He'd seen evil, seen atrocities worse than the human mind could conjure. He knew what true madness looked like.

They sense that about you, chimed in a small voice at the back of Gideon's head. *That's why they draw back from you. That's why they suspect you.*

He shuddered deeply and turned away, trying to compose him.

"I hope you won't let anything stop you in your pursuit of finding this missing girl," Gideon said thickly. "No title, no position, no rank should stop you. Not even mine, do you understand?"

Mr. Foulkes bowed, looking at Gideon with what might have been respect for the first time in a while.

"I will, Lord Rycroft. You have my word on that."

"Good. Now, are there eyewitnesses? Anyone who saw Thomasin, besides her parents, who might be able to say when she was last seen? Come, man. We have an investigation to conduct."

Chapter Eighteen

"It's just that people are talking," Jane Devin said, as tactful and frank as always.

Prudy's heart sank.

Over a week had passed since poor Thomasin Wrecker's disappearance. The whole town and many more people beside had turned up to a church service in silent prayer for Thomasin. The discreet little church was packed to the rafters, and most people had to cluster outside, standing in the cold. A space had been set for Gideon and Prudy in the front row, and Prudy felt guilty sailing past all of the standing people, most of them friends, neighbours, and the extended family of the Wreckers.

The service was as miserable as one might have expected. The young vicar tried his best to keep things positive, but the simple fact was that Thomasin Wrecker had not been found. All of her hopes and dreams lay ahead of her, but now the poor child was missing.

Gideon's face was like stone. He was out from dawn to dusk most days, searching through the woods with other volunteers for any clues that might lead to Thomasin's whereabouts. Whatever free hours he had were spent with the magistrate, questioning as many people as possible.

They ate their meals in silence, and then Gideon staggered upstairs to bed. Prudy didn't press him. He was exhausted. The few conversations they'd exchanged were never encouraging.

"There's simply no leads," Gideon muttered. "More and more people are talking about the Rycroft Hall monster. The thing doesn't exist. How can we chase down a spectre? What do they want me to do – catch some otherworldly creature and bring Thomasin back?"

Prudy had said nothing, only laying a comforting hand on Gideon's forearm. There really wasn't much to say.

Agatha had come home from the market, pinch-faced and angry, muttering something about stupid gossip and fools with nothing better to do than wag their tongues. Prudy had asked her what she meant, and Agatha had mumbled something and gone off.

It was fairly clear what she'd meant, and now Jane Devin had paid an unexpected call.

The two women sat side by side in the parlour, watching the fire flicker in the hearth. The day was unseasonably cold. When Jane had arrived, Prudy had said something about Gideon being out with the magistrate, but Jane had only shook her head.

"It's you I wanted to see," she said firmly.

"I can't imagine how anyone could believe that Gideon had something to do with this awful thing," Prudy murmured. "After all he's done for Dalton Town. He didn't even want to be an earl."

Jane sighed. "People are fickle, my dear. You know that. Gideon... I like him, and Patrick won't hear a word against him, but Gideon simply does not know how to conduct himself. People behaving like you is a skill. I myself do not have it. Gideon ignores the rules of Society in so many ways. It sets him free, but it also leaves him open to censure. I heard a couple of my maids talking about it only this morning, how it was Lord Rycroft that was involved in Thomasin's disappearance."

"Oh, really!"

"Yes, I know, ridiculous. They were both scolded to within an inch of their lives, and I told them that if I heard Lord Rycroft's name on their tongues again, they would be dismissed. But the point is that people are talking about him."

"He's trying so hard to solve the case! He's killing himself over it."

"They see it as guilt, not philanthropy. I hope you don't believe that I'm making any accusations, Prudence. I'm not. I like Gideon, and of course I know he had nothing to do with it. But you must *take* care."

Prudy sighed, raking a hand through her hair. It was knotted up loosely, more to keep it pinned out of the way than out of any real desire to do it up nicely. She hadn't expected guests, and already, she felt comfortable enough with Jane not to worry too much about her appearance.

Was it usual to feel so much at ease around a friend? Prudy knew that if she'd appeared to Cynthia and Blanche in this state, they'd have laughed at her behind their hands and whispered later about how disarranged and blowsy she'd looked.

Not Jane, though. It was a pleasant change.

"A friend already wrote to me, asking if I needed any help," Prudy confessed, eye falling on Cynthia's letter. It sat opened on her writing desk, full of saccharine and thinly veiled curiosity. "I rather felt as though she just wanted to hear some gossip."

Jane sighed. "Well, it's up to you if you want to accept her help, but people *are* talking about it. And about Gideon. Be careful, my dear. Patrick and I speak up for you whenever we can, but since we're known to be your friends, our word is not well listened to."

"I don't want to drag you into this."

"We're friends," Jane said firmly. "We intend to stay by your side until this frightful business is over."

Prudy smiled weakly. "Thank you."

"Now, I brought some food along, just a few little treats to get you by. To bolster your reputation in the community, why not come with me to visit the poor? We bring baskets, and do readings for those who like it, and generally offer a little company and some practical help. Oh, and there's to be a community ball in a few days. The invitations have gone out late, on account of... of everything, but Gideon and you ought to come."

"I'd like that, Jane."

"Excellent." Jane rose to her feet, smiling down at Prudy. "Chin up, my dear. This will pass, after a while."

"It's taking its time," Prudy grumbled.

* * *

The parlour felt a little empty after Jane had gone and Prudy watched the fire for a few long minutes. What would happen if the village turned against them? There was no evidence connecting Gideon to the Thomasin's disappearance, and she knew that he'd been with her all night. But as his wife, how far would her word carry?

There was a sharp rapping at the door, and Prudy jumped. She heard the pattering feet of either Rose or Daisy, hurrying to answer the door. Jane must have forgotten something. A shawl, perhaps, or maybe...

The door creaked open and Daisy slid in, looking nervous.

"A Mr. Isaac Bates for you, your Ladyship."

Prudy scrambled to her feet, sure that she had misheard.

She hadn't.

Isaac stepped into the room after Daisy, beaming.

"Lady Rycroft, I do hope you don't object to my visiting! I volunteered in the search for clues regarding that poor girl's disappearance, and I thought I might trouble you for a cup of tea?"

He was dressed like a country gentleman, although she noticed that his Hessians were remarkably shiny for a man who'd been tramping through the forest. Prudy recovered, politeness winning out.

"Of course, of course. Sit down, please. Daisy, would you bring a tea tray?"

Daisy bobbed a curtsey, shooting a nervous glance at Isaac. The door closed, and the two of them sank into their respective seats. Isaac gave a sigh of relief, stretching out his legs towards the fire.

"What a cosy little room this is. It's quite a domestic scene, is it not?"

Prudy smiled weakly. "Quite. I'm afraid you find my husband not at home, Mr. Bates. He's out helping with the search to find answers."

"Yes, I heard," Isaac commented, inspecting one shiny boot toe. "There is some talk of *too many cooks*, and all that. Perhaps the magistrate ought to be left alone to manage the investigation himself."

Prudy pressed her lips together. It was rude to correct a guest, of course, but she narrowly stopped herself from throwing a cushion at Isaac's head.

"I think it's all hands on deck, as the saying goes," she responded curtly. "Everybody wants to do their part to find Thomasin."

"Quite," Isaac smiled, echoing her sharp response from before. "Well, let's not talk about such miserable subjects, shall we? I've been looking forward to our reunion for quite a while, Lady Rycroft. May I call you Prudence? I know that *Miss Copperwell* won't fit anymore."

Alarm bells rang in the back of Prudy's head. She was busy trying to formulate a response when the door opened, and Agatha, dear Agatha, appeared herself, tea tray in hand. She shot Isaac a none-too-friendly look.

"Your tea, Lady Rycroft," Agatha said smoothly, setting it down. She met Prudy's eye, lifting an eyebrow questioningly. Prudy hoped her expression was properly panicked.

Whatever Agatha saw in Prudy's expression, it must have done the trick. Having poured out two neat cups of tea, Agatha retreated to the corner of the room and took out some sewing with a flourish. Prudy let out a breath she hadn't known she was holding. Thank goodness. Now they were not unaccompanied. Agatha's staid, sensible presence was already making her feel better.

Frowning, Isaac eyed Agatha.

"Can I help you, my good woman?" he asked, in such a grand, overbearing tone that Prudy nearly smashed the teapot over his head.

Agatha, to her credit, did not flinch.

"No, thank you, sir," she responded smoothly.

Annoyed, Isaac faced Prudy again.

"Might we speak in private, Lady Rycroft?"

"We are in private," Prudy responded, widening her eyes as if in confusion.

He bit his lip. "I meant just the two of us."

"It *is* just the two of us. Oh, and Agatha, but anything you can say to me, you can say to Agatha."

Isaac looked even more annoyed at this, but Prudy kept her expression smooth and sweet.

And then – the heavens had smiled on her – a shape limped past the window. Gideon.

"Oh, Gideon is back! Lord Rycroft, I mean. I must go out and greet him," Prudy said, biting back a smile of relief. "Don't hurry yourself out, Mr. Bates, stay and finish your cup of tea, and Agatha or one of the maids will show you out when you're ready to leave. Thank you for calling, and good day to you."

She rose to her feet, Isaac bouncing up also. In that moment, he looked so baffled and miserable that Prudy almost felt sorry for him. He bowed wordlessly, and she took her escape, scurrying out of the parlour. Agatha followed, grim-faced.

"Did that man have an interest in you before you were married?" she asked, voice low.

"I believe so, yes."

149

"Hmph. I don't think you being married has cooled him off."

Prudy sighed. "I was never much interested in him. I do hope he'll get the message soon."

Agatha didn't answer immediately. Instead, she stared at the closed parlour door, worry evident in her face.

"He doesn't strike me as the kind that takes hints easily," she said at last. "But I'll keep an eye on him."

"Thank you, Agatha. I'll go and see Gideon. Perhaps I can coax him to come in for luncheon."

"Right you are, Lady Rycroft."

The two women parted ways, Agatha taking up a seat in the Great Hall to escort Isaac Bates out, and Prudy slipping out of the heavy front door onto the gravel walk outside.

She saw Gideon right away, down by the stables. He was leaning heavily on his stick, deep in conversation with Joseph. His back was turned to her, but she could tell by the set of his thin shoulders that he was exhausted already.

Prudy's chest tightened, the way it had started to do frequently around Gideon. She would have to be a fool not to understand what the feeling meant. It was clearly connected with the way Gideon always seemed to be on her mind, no matter how hard she tried to think of other things. It seemed as though Prudy could not read a page or see a scene without thinking of Gideon's pale, wry face, and wondering what he would say about it.

It was exhausting, and more than a little infuriating. One couldn't *always* be thinking of a wretched man.

The conversation ended, and Joseph moved away. Gideon turned and stopped dead when he saw Prudy. She waved, and he began to walk purposefully towards her. He was not, she noticed, smiling in return, and neither did he wave.

"Good morning, Gideon! I missed you at breakfast. Agatha said you hadn't eaten anything, so perhaps we could take a mouthful of luncheon together."

"What are you doing out here?" Gideon snapped, with no preamble.

It stopped Prudy in her tracks. "What do you mean? I'm just in the garden. This is my home too, I can go wherever I want."

He passed a hand over his face. "Of course it is your home too, I don't dispute that. But at the moment, Thomasin is missing and we don't know what might have happened. Don't you think it would be wiser to stay indoors?"

"I'm only a few feet away from the front door."

"A few feet is all it takes. I mean to talk to Agatha about keeping all the doors and windows locked. She and the maids ought not to go out unaccompanied either. As for you, I'd like you to stay indoors at all times. There's really no need for you to go out."

Prudy blinked. "I... I beg your pardon? You can't forbid me from going outside."

He gave a short laugh. "Oh, but I think I can. I mean it, Prudy. I don't intend to order you around, but this is not a discussion. If you'll excuse me, I have some paperwork to get done this afternoon, then I am going out with Mr. Foulkes again."

And just like that, he stepped past her, hobbling along the gravel walk without so much as a by-your-leave. Prudy was left flabbergasted, standing there alone.

It occurred to her that she ought to warn Gideon that Isaac Bates was in the parlour. After that, they would certainly be having words about this *stay indoors* nonsense.

She stepped into the Great Hall, just in time to see Gideon's coattails disappearing around the corner. Agatha was still sitting where Prudy had left her.

"Has Mr. Bates left?"

"No, Lady Rycroft."

"Hm. It's time he went, I think."

Prudy pushed open the parlour door, ready to politely but firmly escort Isaac Bates out. She was still wondering how she could convey to him that he wasn't really welcome here when the emptiness of the room sank in.

"Mr. Bates?" Prudy asked nervously, as if he might pop out from behind the sofa. No, the man was definitely gone.

Agatha appeared at Prudy's shoulder.

"Well, I never did see anything so odd. He went out through the French doors. Why on earth did he do that? He never passed me."

Prudy eyed the French doors, standing half open, the breeze making the curtains billow, and tried to shake off the feeling of foreboding.

The tea tray and Isaac Bates' cup of tea sat untouched on the table. Steam still curled up from the cup.

He hadn't taken so much as a sip.

Chapter Nineteen

She wasn't going to tell Gideon about Isaac Bates, of course. Prudy had already decided that long before she tapped on his study door.

"Go away, Prudy."

Ignoring him, she pushed open the door. Gideon sat behind his desk, bent over some paperwork. He was scribbling furiously, ink stains already spreading over the white cuffs off his shirt.

"Why am I under house arrest?"

He threw down the pen, leaving nasty blotches all over the paper. Prudy thought it best not to point that out.

"Really? You really have to ask me that? There may be a monster on the loose, Prudence. A real one, not the Rycroft Hall monster people talk about. A person who may have kidnapped Thomasin and a person who kidnaps a girl that age is a special kind of evil."

"So, ordinary crimes do not require evil?"

He sighed. "Of course they do. But to sneak up on a fourteen-year-old girl and abduct her in that way... that is something else. You must see that. What's more, a man who abducts in that way – I'd be willing to bet it is a man, by the way – is likely to choose another girl or young woman as his victim. There's more to an abduction like this than meets the eye. The locals are keeping their womenfolk out of the forest, which is sensible, and I would like you to stay inside. I don't believe that it's too much to ask."

Prudy pulled out a chair and plumped herself down. "I understand your logic, truly I do. But Jane Devin is going out to visit the poor, and I really think..."

"I forbid it."

There was a taut silence. Prudy lifted her eyebrows. "You *forbid* it?"

Gideon had the grace to blush. "I don't mean to curtail your freedom, truly I don't, but this is in your best interests. It's in Jane's best interests, too."

"So you'll condemn her to go about alone? What if she got abducted?"

"Then I would be grateful that you weren't with her, and wonder at Jane, who seems so sensible, going about alone at a time like this."

"Oh, you're impossible."

"I am *rational*," Gideon corrected. "We need to take measures to keep ourselves safe until this abductor is caught."

"And what if he's never caught? What if the hunt lasts for months, and even years? What then?"

Gideon bit his lip. Prudy knew that he had to be thinking, just as she was, about the gossip and rumours springing up, about the filthy looks shot his way, about the older residents surreptitiously throwing up the sign against witchcraft as the Rycroft carriage rumbled by. Her throat tightened at the thought.

She leaned forward, reaching a hand across the desk. If Prudy had hoped that Gideon would match the gesture and take her hand, she was destined to be disappointed.

"We can't cower in our homes," she said softly. "I can take Joseph and one of the maids with me – I don't argue with the logic of not going about alone. But we must consider what will happen if the abductor is not caught. Must we live in fear? And what about the ball?"

He flinched. "Ball? What ball?"

"Jane told me about a community ball, held in town."

"I never go to that."

"Well, I thought we might go this time."

Gideon held her eye for a long moment, and she thought that he might actually be contemplating it.

Then he looked away abruptly, shaking his head.

"It's a bad idea. Besides, we haven't received an invitation."

"We will, Jane said so. I thought we could…"

"We are not going, and that's final."

Prudy clenched her back teeth and forced herself to take a few deep breaths.

"It is *not* final. If I have any say at all here…"

"But you don't, do you?" Gideon snapped, voice raising higher than she'd heard before.

Prudy couldn't help herself. She flinched backwards, whipping her hand off the table. A muscle jumped in Gideon's cheek. He held her gaze for only a few seconds, then hastily looked back down at the papers on his desk. He shuffled them, picking up his pen and putting it down again, tutting at the drying inkblot on one paper.

"You were never meant to be here, need I remind you?" Gideon asked, voice sharp and clipped. "I've tolerated you being here, because you *are* Lady Rycroft. I assumed you'd get bored, and go back to Derby, but you seem determined to stay here. I ought to have been clearer with you from the start. There's really no place for you here. You're looking for a purpose, but there isn't one for you here in the Hall. Dalton Town is a small place, and a lady of the manor simply won't fit. I've often thought that."

"Gideon, I..."

"Please, let me finish," he interrupted. "I think it's important that I be honest with you now. I can't make you leave or stay or indeed do anything you don't want to do, and neither do I intend to lock you up in your room. However, I am Lord Rycroft. If it comes down to it, Agatha and Joseph will obey me over you. Let's not put their loyalty to the test. I have said that you're to stay indoors until the abductor is caught. If you don't like that, you're welcome to leave town at any time you like. You can go back to your family or ask Uncle Bartholomew to set you up somewhere. You'll receive an allowance from me. But in the meantime, if you mean to stay here, I'd like you to do as I say. Do you understand?"

There was a long silence in the room, filled only by the ticking of the clock on the mantelpiece and Gideon's constant shuffling of the papers before him.

"Are you sending me away?" Prudy said, at long last.

Gideon cleared his throat, glancing up at her.

"I think it would be better for everybody if you did go, really. There's no place for you here. You must see that."

Prudy opened her mouth to say that no, she did not see that. She imagined herself having a tantrum, kicking over the chair and breaking things, maybe throwing the heavy glass paperweight at the window. She thought about demanding to know where sweet Gideon was, the man who'd sat with her in a wardrobe all night, let her see his scars and told her the story behind him. Where was the Gideon who'd almost kissed her?

Almost is not enough, she thought suddenly. *He didn't kiss me, after all. Perhaps he wasn't going to. Perhaps I am a silly, gossipy girl who reads too many novels.*

She didn't throw a tantrum, or break anything, and in the end, the words wouldn't come. They queued up on her tongue, angry and tearful and accusing, but Prudy swallowed them down.

"I see," she said finally. "Well, thank you for making everything so very clear to me."

Gideon swallowed hard. He was paler than before, if that was possible. Probably not. Perhaps he was just relieved that he'd finally told Prudy just how unwanted she was here.

Prudy rose to her feet, shaking out her skirts.

"I think I'll skip luncheon today," she said shortly. "But I'm sure Agatha will set the table for you."

"I'm sure," he responded tautly.

Prudy turned on her heel and marched out of the room, closing the door softly behind her even though she wanted to slam it.

She stood outside for a few moments, not sure what to do about the painful ache in her chest.

Abruptly, Agatha came around the corner, clutching a little cream envelope. She stopped short at the sight of Prudy.

"Oh, Lady Rycroft. I was just bringing this note to Lord Rycroft. Looks like an invitation."

"I'll take it to him," Prudy said, before she could even think twice about it. She held out her hand and Agatha gave it to her, entirely trusting.

When the older woman had trotted away around the corner, Prudy broke the seal and pulled out the gilt-edged piece of card inside.

She'd been right. It was an invitation to a community ball, held at the Assembly Rooms in town. Jane had mentioned that 'Assembly Rooms' was a grandiose name for a large, draughty building, but it suited their purpose well enough.

There would be food, dancing, and of course, conversation. The date of the event was the day after tomorrow, at seven o' clock. No RSVPs were needed, only the invitation.

Prudy stood there for a moment, heart thudding. Gideon had said no. Absolutely not. And as Lord Rycroft, he *did* have the final say here.

A wave of anger and misery washed over Prudy.

Have I really been so wrong about him?

Another thought followed it immediately hot with injustice.

Have I really become so weak and vulnerable? Am I like Mama, meekly doing the bidding of a stronger will than mine?

I think not.

Resolved, Prudy slipped the invitation into her pocket, and moved briskly along the hallway away from Gideon's study door. She would write a letter later. Once things were in motion, there wouldn't be anything Gideon could do to stop it.

A dangerous man on the loose or not, Prudy was going to that ball. She would be charming and delightful, and everybody would speak well of her, and Gideon would feel terrible for being so insulting.

Yes, that was it. He'd feel guilty and regretful and do his best to make it up to her.

He'll probably apologise tonight, anyway.

***

It was close to midnight.

Despite herself, Prudy had found that she was tired earlier in the evening, when the dark night closed in, and woke up earlier in the morning, when the sun streamed through her windows.

It felt rather natural, and she didn't wake up groggy or headache-y in the slightest.

Gideon had not come down to supper. Prudy had not intended to go down, to show how displeased she was with his behaviour, but hunger had forced her down.

Besides, he would need an opportunity to apologise, after all.

But Gideon was not down, and Agatha told her that he'd gone out with the magistrate. Prudy sat in the parlour after dinner, quietly seething. Gideon came home shortly after ten o' clock.

He rounded the house, checking doors and windows, and only entered the parlour to double-check the French windows.

Prudy was reminded of Isaac Bates earlier, sneaking out of the French doors, and felt a twinge of unease. But Gideon did not speak to her, except for a cursory *good evening* and then a *good night*, so Prudy did not bother to mention it.

Gideon immediately retired to bed, and there seemed little else for Prudy to do but follow.

The lights were all out downstairs. Bored, she'd wandered to the landing, considering the idea of a midnight snack, but the darkness in the Great Hall dissuaded her. Agatha must have forgotten to light the candles.

She was dressed for bed, naturally, but sat up at the dressing table, eyes on the door.

He must come tonight. He must apologise. Those things he said to me… it can't *be what he truly means.*

But the clock ticked on, and Prudy's hope died away.

Then, at long last, footsteps echoed along the hallway. At first, she thought it was just her imagination, but no, it was definitely footsteps. Heart lifting, Prudy got to her feet.

Slow, even footsteps approached, getting slower and louder until she was quite, quite sure that Gideon was standing outside.

He must be working up the courage to knock, Prudy thought, giddy with relief. If he only knew that she was here, waiting for him to come in?

A second passed, then a minute. Prudy, never the most patient of people, gave in.

"Is that you, Gideon?" she called.

More silence. Frowning, Prudy strode over to the door, flinging it open without preamble.

There was nobody there.

Baffled, she stuck her head out into the hallway, peering up and down. A single candle flickered, and more in the landing along the corridor, but there was no Gideon there. No movement of any sort.

Prudy swallowed hard. She closed the door firmly, and after a moment's thought, locked it afterwards and then went to bed.

Chapter Twenty

If Jane and Patrick were surprised when Prudy met them at the gate, instead of having their carriage come into the courtyard to turn around, they did not show it. They gamely turned the carriage around there, in the entryway, although of course it was an odd request on Prudy's part.

She climbed into the carriage quickly, resisting the urge to glance back at the house like a guilty child. She was *not* going to be made to feel silly and small in her own home. And this *was* her home, regardless of what Gideon had said about her not belonging here.

I will belong. I will belong. I can find my place.

Prudy was a little out of breath, reeling at her own daring and, like a child, terrified of being caught.

She was fairly sure that Gideon was not at home. There was a thin beam of light coming from underneath his study door, but he often left a candle burning when he was out, more from carelessness than anything. Joseph was off somewhere, Agatha was down in the kitchen, and heaven only knew where the girls were.

Prudy had been able to dress herself up her in room, wriggling into one of her more fitted gowns and pinning up her hair herself with only a little help from Daisy, who seemed eager to take part with her mistress in a secret. Really, she did a good job of it, good enough to present herself as Lady Rycroft at a community ball.

I still feel as though I'm play-acting as a real lady. The wife of an earl. Me. Hard to imagine.

Jane shuffled aside in the carriage to make room for Prudy, smiling at her.

"I'm so glad you could come after all, my dear. You'll like the ball, I think. The Assembly Rooms aren't particularly fancy, but they always look lovely. Lots of decorations and candles, and so on."

"It's a pity Gideon couldn't come," Patrick chimed in. "I knew he wouldn't like the idea of it, but... well. I'm not surprised he got a cold, after all that traipsing around in the damp forest."

It took Prudy a minute to recall that a cold was the excuse

she'd used to explain away Gideon's absence. Her letter to Jane had been brief, dashed off in a hurry before she could lose her nerve.

"Yes, but I'm sure he'll come around soon," Prudy lied neatly.

Well, it might *not* be a lie. She hadn't seen Gideon at all during the past day or two since their argument, so he might well have caught a cold.

The carriage rumbled through the dark forest. The wind whipped around them, but there was no sign of rain – or, heaven forbid, thunder and lightning – so far.

It wasn't such a terrible thing, was it? She was Gideon's wife, not his servant. He couldn't order her around the way he had. It simply wasn't fair. This would show him that she wasn't to be dictated to.

It's for his own wretched good after all. I have to be the benevolent lady, I have to prove to the locals that we're good people, that we are to be trusted, that Gideon would never, never...

She swallowed hard, not wanting to even consider the crime people believed Gideon could be guilty of. It wasn't *fair*.

The forest pathway opened up onto a cobbled road. There were a couple of other carriages on the road ahead of them, lanterns bobbing along. Up ahead, she spotted a large building which could only be the Assembly Rooms, windows glimmering with light. Prudy shifted, peering out of the window, and felt a kernel of excitement start up inside her.

She'd always loved parties, hadn't she? Cynthia would be there – and Blanche was here on a visit, and they could chat and laugh together like old times. Catherine wouldn't be there, but it was a start, wasn't it?

Jane leaned forward, attracting Prudy's attention.

"Try and enjoy yourself," she said quietly. "You deserve a nice night. There'll be food and drink and dancing, and lots of conversation. Lots of new people to meet, and a great many you already met at your party. How are you feeling?"

"A little nervous," Prudy admitted. The carriage rolled to a halt in front of the Assembly Rooms, and they climbed out, one by one.

Groups of people were making their way up the steps,

chattering and laughing. A wall of warmth hit her as soon as they stepped over the threshold. Already, some musicians were starting up, strains of fiddle and flute music drifting through the room. Jane snatched up two champagne glasses.

"One for me, and one for Prudy, I'm afraid, Patrick," she said, smiling at her husband. "I only have two hands."

He made some clever comment back that made Jane laugh, eyes sparkling as she looked up at her husband.

Prudy had stopped listening. She was suddenly aware that the noise and warmth and laughter seemed rather tinny to her now, because all she wanted was to have Gideon beside her.

I miss the wretched man, she thought, heart sinking into her stomach. *I shouldn't have come, and I miss him. I wish he were here. What am I going to do?*

***

"... and then I said, Miss Cleeves, you really can*not* wear pink. No, I'm sorry, I cannot allow you to keep wearing that gown. If I were you, I'd leave at once. It's for the best. And leave she did, and didn't dance with Lord Bryne again that night." Cynthia finished, with a triumphant nod at her friends. She drained her champagne glass and gestured for the footman to bring her another.

"You are ever so forthright, Cynthia," Blanche gushed. The other girls all tittered among themselves, apparently thrilled by Cynthia's scathing put-down of her rival.

Prudy smothered a yawn.

The ball was going reasonably well. There'd been a spate of dancing, but prospects were slim and Prudy didn't particularly want to dance with any of them. She'd pleaded a twisted ankle early on, and that saved her from having to accept any further offers of dancing. Isaac Bates was there, of course, and had asked her to dance three times. She'd refused all three times, much to his annoyance. He seemed to have left her alone by now, although she knew he hadn't left.

So that had left her with the option of conversation with her acquaintances, and not much else. The chat with her friends she'd so looked forward to now seemed rather... well, trite.

161

More than trite.

Ridiculous. Stupid. A little cruel, even.

"Oh, Cynthia, do take a look at that gown over there!" chimed in one Miss Amanda Cooke. She was a thin, hook-nosed young woman with an elegant taste in fashion and a tremendous fortune behind her.

Prudy had met her for the first time that day and would be pretty happy not to meet her ever again.

The ladies all looked, and immediately broke into titters.

"What *does* she think she looks like?" Blanche gasped. "Blue? With that skin? Oh, and it's last season's style, too. For shame, for shame."

"I reckon she did her own hair, too. Awful, isn't it?"

"I know her. She's an interfering old busybody, too dull to gossip properly or *do* anything exciting."

"The thing about the ugly gown and last season's hair," Cynthia said slowly and thoughtfully, "is that a lady can get away with it if she's pretty enough. I've known women with bad dresses and hardly any money snap up lords and barons just because they are beautiful. That's this woman's real crime – she's *plain*."

There were giggles at this witticism. Sighing, Prudy turned to look at this unfortunate woman. She froze.

Jane Devin stood there, arm in arm with Patrick, chatting to another couple. Jane, in a blue dress, with her simply done hair.

Prudy stiffened. "That's not kind, Cynthia."

There was a brief pause at that.

"I beg your pardon?" Cynthia managed.

"I know her. That's Mrs Jane Devin. She's very nice."

Miss Amanda snickered. "Oh? And you didn't advise against that gown? Shocking, my dear Lady Rycroft."

"She's my friend," Prudy said, a little more sharply than she'd intended. Miss Amanda pinkened, shooting Prudy a quick glance of dislike.

There were a few moments of awkward silence. Blanche, at last, cleared her throat and said something or other about the quality of the champagne.

Nobody said anything more about Jane, at the very least.

Prudy sat back in her seat and stopped listening to the conversation for a little while. For the past hour or so, she had come to the miserable realisation that she was not having a good time. Perhaps it was the company of her old friends, or perhaps it was something else.

She wasn't willing to let herself consider that it might be Gideon's absence. After all, he'd made it clear that he didn't want her here.

But he couldn't mean that, could he? No, he couldn't. He'd apologise sooner or later, or else... or else it would be smoothed over somehow. It must be! This couldn't be the end of it.

A lump rose to Prudy's throat, and childish tears pricked at her eyes. There was nobody she could talk to about it. If she'd been considering telling Cynthia about it, even about some of it, those ideas were entirely gone now.

"Now, what *I* want to know," Miss Amanda suddenly said, leaning forward with a snake-like smile that did not quite reach her eyes, "is whether that business at Rycroft Hall is all sorted. You must know something, Lady Rycroft."

There was a heartbeat of silence.

"You mean the disappearance?" Blanche asked, barrelling in with her usual bluntness. "That little girl who disappeared or rather that was abducted? Awful, wasn't it? Like something out of a novel."

Prudy pressed her lips together. "Yes, it is awful. It didn't happen at the Hall, but near the town well."

"Oh? Isn't the well on Rycroft land?" Miss Amanda mused, tapping one perfect fingernail against her chin. "I heard that Lord Rycroft wanders around in the night. Sleepwalking, is it?"

"No, he just likes to take the night air," Prudy responded, before she could stop herself. After all, that sounded much worse.

Cynthia and Blanche exchanged looks but stayed silent.

"And there's no leads on the case?" Miss Amanda pressed. Prudy was beginning to dislike the woman immensely. She was cursing herself for not escaping when she could. She could be having a nice conversation with Jane, about less uncomfortable topics.

"No," she responded, hoping that her short and pointedly unfriendly answer would put the wretched woman off asking more.

She should have known better, really.

Miss Amanda beamed, scenting blood.

"*Oh*? I hear, too that Lord Rycroft is *very* involved in the case. Odd, don't you think?"

"Why would it be odd?" Prudy snapped. "A terrible crime has taken place, and you ask why my husband is so keen to solve it? Disappearances like that leading to possible abductions are vile things anyway, the community is reeling. I'm not sure why you should think it odd."

Miss Amanda leaned forward, pursing her lips. "Well, there are rumours... forgive me, Lady Rycroft, but it cannot be denied that your husband is *odd*, isn't that so? It is said that he... he has rather *unusual* habits."

Another tight silence. Prudy swallowed hard, forcing herself not to look away from Miss Amanda's bright, gleeful eyes.

"What are you implying, Miss Amanda?"

"Implying? Me? Nothing, I assure you. I only wonder... well, one can't *help* but wonder whether Lord Rycroft might have seen something, or else... well, or might know more than he's letting on."

Prudy allowed herself to indulge in a brief fantasy of dashing her half-finished glass of champagne into Miss Amanda's face.

Although, why allow it to just be a fantasy?

"I think I've heard quite enough of this sort of thing," Prudy said at last, voice slow and angry. "I'm tired of hearing your implications, Miss Amanda."

"Oh, I never meant..."

"Yes, yes you did," Prudy interrupted, voice rising louder than it really should in such a genteel gathering. "You meant every word of it. You're so hungry for gossip, all of you, don't care to think about whether it's kind or not."

Cynthia gave a short laugh. "To hear this from *you*, Prudy..."

Prudy rounded on her. "I'll thank you to keep quiet, Cynthia! I've had quite enough of you."

To do her credit, Cynthia had the sense to keep silent after that.

That left Prudy free to turn back to Amanda. More and more people were falling silent, glancing their way, but Prudy was too angry to notice.

"For your information, Miss Amanda, I am Lady Rycroft, not

you. I know exactly what's going on in my house and my land, and I know that my husband had nothing to do with this situation. Oh, that's what you're all saying, isn't it? That Lord Rycroft is behind this disappearance. Well, I can assure you that he isn't. He's a fine man, one I love with all my heart, and I was with him *all night* the night that poor child disappeared, do you hear me?"

There was a pause after that. Prudy realized that everything was quiet all around. The entire room had fallen silent, and everybody was looking at her.

Colour rose to her cheeks. She could almost hear the echo of her own angry voice bouncing around the room. Almost on the brink of asking why everybody was looking at her – as if she didn't know – Prudy happened to turn around to where the door was, behind her, and saw at once why everybody was staring.

The door had been flung wide open, a curl of night air and rain smattering inside. The heat of the room was so intense that Prudy hadn't felt the draft until right now.

And of course, that wasn't all.

A man stood in the doorway.

Gideon.

It had clearly been raining, and Gideon's hair was curling damply around his forehead. His cravat was limp, and his shoulders dark from rain. Water pooled around his feet and dripped from the hem of his coat onto the floor. He wore muddy boots and tight riding breeches, his dark, old-fashioned coat giving him the look of a pale, dark Gothic hero.

No, not a hero. A *villain*. She had always liked the villains better, anyway.

He didn't have his cane, and his limp was barely noticeable when he strode across the room towards her.

"Gideon," Prudy gasped.

"Prudence."

"What are you doing here?"

"I could ask you the same."

Prudy glanced around, suddenly aware that just about everybody in the room was deathly quiet, listening into their conversation.

"I told you," Gideon said, voice dropping low, "not to leave the house unaccompanied. Do you think I did it just to curtail your freedom? No, I required it of you because there's a dangerous man on the loose."

"How did you get here?" was all Prudy could manage. "It's dark, and raining, and…"

And your leg, was what she didn't quite allow herself to say. Probably for the best.

Gideon gave a twisted smile. "You wanted to ride Cicero, didn't you? Well, now is your chance. Come on, dear. We're going."

He reached out and grabbed Prudy's wrist. Turning on his heel, he stormed back out of the door without so much as glancing at anybody, and hauled her along after him.

Gideon was stronger than Prudy had imagined. She allowed herself to be yanked along for a few steps, more out of shock than anything else. The cold hit her like a wall as they crossed the threshold, and a mist of rain landed on her, thick as a blanket, making her gasp.

"My shawl…"

"Jane will bring it," Gideon shot back, not even glancing over his shoulder at her.

This, more than anything else, shocked Prudy out of her stupor. She dug in her heels, trying to pull her wrist free. She could see Cicero standing in the courtyard, near the line of carriages.

Gideon let go of her arm, and Prudy staggered backwards, almost overbalancing.

"What do you think you're doing?" she snapped. "You just humiliated me in front of everybody."

"Oh? Well, I'm sorry, but I'm not going to have Lady Rycroft added to the list of missing people. You may not like me, Prudy, and we didn't choose to be married, but I'm not going to see you hurt or worse, abducted. Don't you think that this person, whoever he is, will be attracted to this gathering?"

"Well, I…"

"I asked you not to come here."

"No, Gideon, you *told* me not to come here. I'm not Agatha. You can't order me around. I'm your wife, and I'll do as I please."

Gideon clenched his fists by his sides. "You really don't see the danger, do you?"

There was a brief silence after that.

"Are you going to go back in?" Gideon said, his voice quiet over the increasing drum of the rain. "I'm not going to drag you out again, if that's what you're afraid of."

Prudy let out a long breath. The energy had drained out of her. The cold was creeping in.

"I'll come home," she muttered. "And I'll make preparations to leave in the morning."

Gideon flinched as if from a blow.

"Good," he said sharply. "That's good."

Chapter Twenty-One

Gideon suspected that riding Cicero was more nerve-wracking than Prudy had expected. She clung tight to him, arms around his waist.

Any other time, he might have felt pleased at himself to drawing her this close to him. There might have been something like elation, and pride at being able to control such a fantastic beast as Cicero.

Tonight, though, Gideon only felt hollow.

"I'll come home, and I'll make preparations to leave in the morning."

That was what he'd wanted, wasn't it? He wanted Prudy to leave. It was better for everybody, not least of all, her. This was the best outcome – the inevitable outcome, really, when one really got down to it. She was always going to leave. Leave this place, leave her new life, leave him.

None of this was what she wanted. *He* wasn't what she wanted.

In time, he was sure, the pain of departure would stop bothering either of them.

For now, however, it hurt more than Gideon could ever have imagined.

Prudy slid off the back of the saddle before Cicero had even come fully to a stop.

"Goodnight," she said frankly. Dully.

Gideon sat on the back of the horse, rain pelting down and soaking him to the bone, and watched her go into the house. Up until now, Prudy was always the one who seemed to be driving them closer together. She tried to talk to him, tried to organize things, tried to get him to have dinner with her and go places. It had always been her pulling, and him pulling away.

It seemed as though she'd given up.

Why didn't he feel more relieved?

Joseph came running out in the rain, a wide-brimmed hat shielding his face from the weather.

"Agatha and the girls went down into the town," he said, voice pitched above the patter of rain. "Daisy's mother is sick, and they didn't want to go alone, what with a dangerous person around. It's just me here, your lordship."

"Quite right for them to go together," Gideon responded, sliding off the horse. His bad leg twinged as he hit the ground, and he bit back a grimace of pain. "Give Cicero a good seeing-to, won't you? He's cold and wet. Then you can retire for the night."

"Right you are, your lordship."

Joseph took the reins and led Cicero around the corner of the house, towards the stables, and no doubt from there to the little cottage which was Joseph's home – which he'd long wanted to share with Agatha, if Gideon wasn't mistaken – and out of sight.

Gideon was left to limp into the house alone, his wet clothes weighing him down.

Inside, the Great Hall was colder than ever. There were hardly any candles burning, which was unusual considering Prudy's love of light. He wondered if she'd snuffed them out in temper, or whether she simply hadn't bothered to light them at all. If she'd given up.

His leg ached painfully as he crossed the Hall towards his study, wet clothes sticking to him and chafing his skin. He needed a change of clothes, but the stairs loomed high and difficult to climb at that moment. He wasn't sure he had the energy.

What was more, Gideon knew in his heart that if he climbed the stairs to his room, he would cross the landing and head towards Prudy's room.

She deserves an explanation.

He squeezed his eyes shut.

Gideon's study was much the same as how he'd left it, candle burning and all. His papers were shuffled about his desk, disordered, and he knew he hadn't left them like that. Probably Rose or Daisy, tidying clumsily in here. He would have to have a word with Agatha about that.

Tumbling into his seat, Gideon found no respite from his whirling mind and the discomfort throbbing through his body.

I was wrong. Wrong to drag her away like that.

The fear Gideon had felt when he discovered Prudy's room and parlour empty was still singing through his veins, along with the humiliation of finally hearing the story stammered from Daisy.

Prudy had been clever enough not to involve Agatha, judging by the woman's stony expression.

I should apologise. I should explain.

Gideon stared at the closed inside door of his study and willed himself to get up and open it.

***

Prudy didn't allow herself to cry. She could cry tonight, under her covers, and be composed in time to get up in the morning and climb into the Rycroft carriage.

I'm glad I'm leaving this place, she tried to tell herself. *I'm glad I'm leaving him.*

It wouldn't stick, though. It didn't help that the wretched man was so *attractive* to her, even when showing up in the doorway of a ballroom wet and dishevelled and angry, like a Gothic villain.

Prudy yanked a bag out from her wardrobe and began stuffing things at random into it. It felt good to be doing something. She hadn't seen any of the servants, and after the trick she'd pulled on Gideon, doubtless Agatha wouldn't want to talk to her again.

Thank goodness I'm leaving, Prudy thought again, listlessly.

It didn't stick.

And then there came a tentative knocking on the door.

Prudy's breath hitched in her throat, eyes widening.

It was Gideon. Of course it was Gideon. He could only be here to apologize, to say that he hadn't meant for her to go, that he *did* care about her, he *did*...

Prudy had flown to the door before she even decided to do it, yanking it open.

Everything was going to be alright. She wouldn't have to leave, Gideon would finally *see* her, and...

And Isaac Bates stood smiling in the doorway.

Prudy blinked, as if that might rearrange the scene before her into something more sensible.

"There you are, Prudy," Isaac said, his smile stretching his face wide. "Are you happy to see me?"

Releasing the doorknob, Prudy backed away. That was a

mistake, because Isaac advanced then, crossing into the room. For the first time, she noticed the glimmer of a long, silver-bladed chef's knife in his hand.

Fear closed its long fingers over Prudy's heart then, freezing her in place.

"Isaac, what..."

"Oh, this? Ah, I just thought it was better to be safe than sorry, don't you think? In case that troublesome Lord Rycroft or his minions got in our way. I came for you, Prudy. You must have known I would."

Prudy managed to unfasten her feet from the floor, and backed rapidly away, trying to put a soft armchair between Isaac and herself.

Isaac didn't even break her gaze. He turned the knife handle absently in his fingers.

"We should leave soon," he said after a pause. "Before that so-called husband of yours discovers that I'm here."

"Isaac, I... I'm sorry if I gave you the wrong impression, but I am married. You must know that."

"I do," Isaac said, a trifle defensively. "But you and I are meant to be together. I won't let anything get in our way. I've fancied myself in love before, and those women have always been... *disappointing*. But not you. You're perfect. You're charming, and friendly, and social, and you're pretty, too. So colourful. We'll make an excellent team together, you and me. You only need to take your destiny in your hands and follow me."

It sounded like he'd ripped the words right out of a novel. Maybe he had. Swallowing hard, Prudy backed away further, until the edge of her dressing-table bumped against her back.

Isaac kept coming, until he was only a few inches away from her.

She could see how the shoulders of his coat were drenched with rain, could smell the peaty night-air scent coming off him. His hair was greasy and unkempt, somehow even worse than when she'd seen him only hours before at the party, and his eyes were bloodshot.

Prudy gulped, trying to simultaneously keep an eye on his face and on his knife.

"Isaac, if I've made you think otherwise, I am sorry, but..."

"I saw how he dragged you away from the ball," Isaac interrupted. "Such a man isn't worthy of you. But me... I am worthy of you. You have no idea what I've done to keep our future together intact. What I *will* do."

A cold feeling snaked down Prudy's spine. "What... what have you done?" she stammered.

Isaac sighed. "A girl saw me coming back from the house. I had to keep an eye on you, you see. She was going to tell people, and I simply wasn't ready to let it all come out yet. I cared for *you*, you see, and your reputation."

Prudy felt sick. "Thomasin Wrecker. She saw you, and you stalked her. And then she disappeared."

Isaac shrugged idly. "Oh, I don't know her name. It doesn't matter."

"It doesn't *matter*? A child is missing, and it doesn't *matter*? How can you say that?"

Prudy tore away from him, drawing in deep, ragged breaths.

"Did you hurt her? You're a monster! A vile, horrible monster, and I could never have loved you!"

In hindsight, that was a silly thing to say to a madman wielding a knife.

Isaac's expression hardened. "You don't know what you're saying, Prudy."

A macabre dance started up, with Prudy retreating around the room and Isaac advancing, him somehow always managing to stay between her and the door. He held his knife a little differently now, angled back towards his forearm, ready to stab with frightening power.

"Oh, Prudy," he said, sounding genuinely disappointed. "Don't say I was wrong about you. Don't say that you're just like all the others."

"Others?" Prudy gasped.

He shook his head, a glazed look coming to his eyes.

"They were irrelevant, I see that now. Servants and farmer's daughters and like, not *ladies*. Not like you. That's why I thought you were different, but perhaps I was wrong. Oh, do say I wasn't wrong."

Prudy had read a great many novels, like most other girls her age, and there was always a moment when the heroine was confronted by the villain. The man might have various motivations – love, lust, greed, and so on – and the hero and her integrity always had to comport herself with dignity, wit, and resignation.

Or, of course, she could swoon.

Prudy would have liked to have fainted. It would solve some of her immediate problems, at the very least.

Unfortunately for her, although her chest tightened with fear, it seemed that fainting away altogether was simply not an option. She swayed on her feet, but mostly stayed on them.

Isaac lifted the knife, blade glittering, until it was only inches away from Prudy's chin.

"Yes, I see now that I've made a mistake," he murmured. "You've been false to me, haven't you? You promised the world, then you married Lord Rycroft. Fickle, heartless, and foolish, like all the other women. What a disappointment."

Prudy opened her mouth to speak, no doubt about to say something endlessly stupid and earn herself a slit throat right away.

And then there was a gasp from the doorway.

"Prudy! And... who are you?"

They both whirled around.

Gideon stood there, mouth agape, his walking-stick loose in his hand.

Prudy was in the perfect position to see Isaac's face lose all semblance of humanity, curdling into something cruel and vengeful and quite, quite mad.

"He's got a knife!" Prudy yelped, just before Isaac seized her shoulder and shoved her backwards with all his considerable strength.

She went flying backwards, tipping head-over-heels over the dressing table and landing on the floor with a *crash* that knocked the breath out of her body.

Isaac sprinted towards Gideon, knife glittering. Prudy didn't have breath to scream, although to her credit, she tried.

Gideon swung his cane, faster than Prudy might have thought possible. It struck Isaac across the head with an echoing *crack*, and the man staggered to one side, nearly dropping his knife.

He recovered, lunging at Gideon. This time, he hit him low in the chest, and the two men went down.

Prudy managed a gurgling cry, crawling to her hands and knees. Her chest ached horribly and there was a sharp pain in her side. Where had her breath gone? Her lungs felt like deflated sacks.

On the floor, Isaac and Gideon were twisting around, a macabre image of two boys playing at wrestling. The knife glinted, and Isaac brought it down hard towards Gideon's chest. Prudy's scream caught in her throat.

Gideon's hand wrapped around Isaac's wrists, those pale, slim fingers stronger than she could ever have imagined. His arms flexed, and suddenly Isaac shot backwards, and Gideon was on top of him, tilted to one side to ease the burden on his bad leg.

Isaac's teeth were clenched, lips drawn back like an animal. Gideon's expression was icy and grim. Focused.

Like a soldier.

And then Gideon stretched out his hand, snatching up his cane, and brought the heavy handle down on Isaac's head.

Crunch.

The sound was sickening. The colour drained from Isaac's face and his eyes rolled back, expression going slack.

Gideon backed away, gasping for breath, walking stick still clutched in his hands.

"Get me something to tie his hands," he rasped.

Still breathless, Prudy scuttled to obey. She took up the cord used to tie the curtains, limping over to Gideon.

With shocking ease, Gideon rolled Isaac over onto his back, tying his hands securely with the cord.

"He... he's been following me," Prudy managed. Her voice sounded thick. "I had no idea. I... I knew that he had a fancy for me when we were at home, but I never thought... I never imagined this, Gideon!"

"I know," Gideon responded shortly. "You were never to blame. We are lucky he didn't do more damage."

Prudy's eyes fluttered closed. "You don't know what he's already done."

Gideon stiffened. "What has he done?"

"He is responsible for Thomasin Wrecker's disappearance."

There was a taut silence. Gideon swore under his breath, drawing the back of his hand across his forehead.

"What a mess," he managed at last. "Prudy, would you fetch Joseph, please? He will either be in the stables or in his cottage. Agatha and the girls are out."

Prudy nodded tightly, turning to go. There'd be no rest for either of them tonight. Isaac would need to be secured properly. He would come around soon, and who only knew what state he would be in. The magistrate would need to be summoned. Questions must be asked. It would be a long night, for sure. Poor Agatha and the girls would return to chaos.

"And... and Prudence?"

She stopped in the doorway, leaning against it for strength, and glanced back over her shoulder. Gideon was hunched over with his back to her, seeming almost drained of energy.

"Yes?"

"Unless... unless you particularly want to leave, I wonder whether it would be a good idea for you not to leave tomorrow. You... you'll need to rest and recover, after all. You've had a shock, after all. Another few minutes, and I think he might really have done you some harm."

Prudy bit her lip. "I think you're right. I will stay."

He let out a sigh, almost one of relief, although she couldn't see his face to decide for certain.

"That's good. Thank you, Prudy."

Chapter Twenty-Two

Of course, nobody could talk about anything other than the Rycroft Hall Incident, as it was being christened.

Visitors and well-wishers had turned up to the Hall in their dozens, all to be firmly turned away by Agatha. A couple of visitors got through – Jane and Patrick Devin, of course, the officious Mr. Foulkes, and even Cynthia and Blanche.

Prudy supposed she was still friends with them. There were worse sins in life than gossiping, anyway. Cynthia had even made an effort to invite Jane to some of her parties, so perhaps Prudy's hot-tempered words had been taken to heart.

Or so she hoped.

Neither Prudy nor Gideon had escaped unscathed, in more ways than one. Gideon's slim, pointed nose had been broken, and was healing up with a faint bump in the bridge. He had moaned over it, staring in the mirror, but Prudy had announced that she thought it rather rakish and handsome.

Gideon had gone red at that, but of course a man as pale as him, was always going to blush easily.

The stabbing pain in Prudy's side had been identified as a broken rib. There was little the doctor could do, beside prescribing rest and advising she leave off corsets for a while.

Prudy did not need to be told twice.

The two of them were sitting in Prudy's parlour now – she supposed it was *their* parlour these days, rather than just hers – being fussed over by Agatha.

Isaac's invasion of the house had shaken the servants, too. Each one of them blamed themselves, since it seemed that Isaac Bates had hardly ever left the house at all, flitting between unused rooms and hiding in the cellar. Out in the country, it wasn't considered necessary to lock one's doors and windows *all* the time.

Prudy heard no more footsteps outside her bedroom door at night, although she lay up most nights listening for them, on edge to hear Isaac Bates trudging up and down the hallway.

With time, she supposed the fear would rescind. It had

shaken most of the town.

Isaac, was brought before the magistrate, accused of abducting Thomasin Wrecker. The evidence against him was overwhelming, and despite his protests of innocence, he was swiftly found guilty.

The search for Thomasin Wrecker had been extensive, with Prudy leading the charge to find the missing girl. It was her determination and bravery that eventually led to the discovery of Thomasin, locked away in a remote cabin in the woods. The villagers rejoiced at her safe return, and Thomasin was reunited with her family, albeit shaken and traumatized by the ordeal. Isaac's punishment served as closure for the community, a reminder of the consequences of such despicable acts. And as he was led away to face his punishment, Prudy couldn't help but feel a sense of relief that justice had been served.

***

"I got a letter from your father today," Gideon said abruptly.

He was sitting beside her on the sofa, both of their legs propped up on footstools, as Agatha had insisted, blankets draped over them.

"Oh?" Prudy blinked, suddenly remembering that she *did* have a family and a life beyond the walls of Rycroft Hall.

"They're concerned, obviously. Your father said that your sister, Catherine, is coming, whether we want her to or not." He chuckled, shaking his head. "Of course, she's welcome. I'll ask Agatha to make her up a room, if she's not too busy spending time with Joseph these days."

"Agatha and Joseph? What do you mean?"

Gideon gave a small smile and shook his head again. "Oh, nothing. Just something I've noticed. They've known each other for a long time, after all. Are you looking forward to seeing your sister?"

"I certainly am," Prudy said, smiling. "I've missed her. And it *will* be nice to show off my fine, beautiful house, I think."

"Certainly."

There was a little pause after that, a pleasantly comfortable silence, broken only by the crackle of the fire. Outside, Prudy could

177

hear the slop of a mop on the floor of the Great Hall. It was oddly soothing.

"I owe you an apology," Gideon said abruptly.

She shifted to look at him. "Oh?"

"I think you know what for."

"For turning up at a ball, wet and angry like a Gothic hero, then dragging me out into the night like a Gothic villain?"

He grimaced. "Yes, I do mean that. Patrick said I made a fool of myself and you. I think I was too angry to see it at the time. I never meant to order you around like a tyrant. Truly, I did only care about your safety."

Prudy bit her lip. "You had a point about my safety, I will confess. It's just... well, I've had a lifetime of curtailed freedom, dancing to the tune of my family, and being Lady Rycroft is... well, it's rather heady."

He smiled wryly. "I can imagine. But you deserved better, especially after..." he trailed off, gesturing to himself. "The scars. You saw them, and... you were gracious."

"I don't know what monsters you've been spending time with," Prudy said frankly, "but those scars don't make you less of a man. They're a sign of how strong you are, and how much you can endure. You ought to be proud of them."

"It's not just the scars," he murmured. "It's not just my skin that was damaged. It was my mind, too. I don't sleep at night because of nightmares. The thing about nightmares is that you can tell yourself they aren't real when you wake up. But I can't do that, because what I see in my dreams was real. The war changed me. I wasn't the same man when I came back, and a great many of my friends simply could not handle it. I suppose I shouldn't blame them. But it was easier to lock myself away, and solitude became comfortable. That was one of the reasons why I was so keen that you should leave. Isolation is terribly lonely, but it is, at least, predictable. I'm sorry. I treated you poorly. In fact, I don't think I realised just how badly I wanted you to stay here with me until you finally told me you were leaving."

Prudy swallowed back a lump in her throat. She shifted in her seat so that she was facing Gideon properly.

"And *do* you want me to stay?" she asked quietly.

He nodded slowly, reaching out tentatively for her hand.

Prudence met him halfway, their fingers lacing together.

It seemed to be the easiest and most natural thing in the world.

"When I first came here, to Rycroft Hall," Gideon said in a rush, "I wanted to help the locals without interacting with them too much. I knew that they were afraid of being punished for poaching but were also going without thinking when it came to meat. So, I would shoot a few rabbits, things like that, and leave the meat where the locals could get it. I thought I was being helpful. Instead, a rumour sprang up about a monster, the Rycroft Hall monster, feasting on animals, killing for the sake of it and leaving the corpses. It was macabre. That was when I began to understand just how far removed I had become from other people, how little I understood them."

"It was you," Prudy breathed. "You started the rumour."

He sighed. "I'm afraid so. I stopped leaving meat for the locals — not that there was much to start with — but the gossip persisted. My point is, Prudy, I'm something of a fool. I have good intentions, but I always seem to make mistakes. I try to be a good man, but I can never seem to fit into the mould Society has set out for me."

She bit her lip, guilty recollections of the gossipy comments she and her friends had shared.

"I shouldn't worry about that if I were you," she said at last. "Society isn't particularly kind to its own. It's better to be your own person, I think. You'll be censured either way."

"Thank you, Prudy. That means a lot. There's been something I've wanted to tell you for a while, but I felt as though I couldn't. Not since kicking up such a fuss about you being here."

"Oh? Well, you might as well tell me. Agatha won't let us lift a finger in the house, so we have a great deal of time for conversation."

Gideon drew in a breath. "Will you marry me, Prudy?"

There was a brief silence.

"My dear," Prudy said softly, "perhaps you weren't aware, but we're *already* married."

He smiled, a tight little curl of his lips that made Prudy's heart flutter more than it should.

"I married a Miss Prudence Copperwell, certainly. I hardly

knew her. But now I think I would like to embark on proper married life with a young woman who's captured my heart — I didn't even think I had one — and her name is Lady Prudy Rycroft."

"An entirely different person," Prudy agreed, nodding solemnly.

"Well, there are some differences." Gideon cleared his throat awkwardly. "I'm trying to say, Prudy, that I think I am falling in love with you."

Prudy sucked in a breath, eyes wide. Gideon was meeting her eye diligently, waiting for her to respond. Their fingers were still laced together.

On impulse — ignoring the sharp pain in her side — Prudy leaned forward, closing the gap between them. Hardly able to contemplate her own daring, she fitted her lips to Gideon's, hearing his surprised gasp.

She'd never kissed anyone before, naturally.

Well, nobody can complain, Prudy thought. *After all, I am kissing my* husband.

An odd feeling of warmth spread all down her chest, curling around her heart and almost *tingling* there.

She pulled back, and Gideon lifted his hand, tracing her jaw with his fingertips.

"I must tell you, Lord Rycroft, your sentiments are entirely returned," she murmured.

Epilogue

Now this, Prudy thought happily, *is a real wedding.*

They had thrown open the doors of Rycroft Hall, inviting all the locals as well as friends from further afield. This time, Agatha had enlisted half a dozen women from the town to help with cooking, and roughly the same amount of men to act as footmen.

Maybe we should take on more staff, Prudy thought, smiling as she passed Joseph, bearing a tray of champagne flutes. They'd certainly need more when Joseph and Agatha went away for their honeymoon. She wasn't particularly surprised when the two middle-aged servants shyly announced their engagement, and Gideon wasn't surprised, either.

Apparently, it had been coming for a while.

Jane and Patrick stood arm in arm in the corner, laughing about something, the very image of wedded bliss. Cynthia was gliding here and there, eyes sharp for an eligible gentleman to pounce upon. Blanche was around somewhere.

And there, tucked in a corner as usual, stood Gideon. He had that odd smile on his face, that thrilling little curl that always made Prudy's insides flutter in a way she'd never thought they could.

Before she could go over to her husband – and that word had real meaning to it now – an arm slipped through hers.

"Congratulations on your wedding, sister," Catherine said, grinning. "I feel as though I can say it and mean it, now."

"Well, I actually *do* feel married now," Prudy confessed. The two sisters pulled away from the crowded ballroom, seeking out a quieter spot to talk. "I half expected you to bring Simon along."

Catherine gave a quick little smile. "We're engaged, you know. It's not *quite* official, but the banns will be read soon. Papa won't put it in the *Gazette*, but you know I don't care about that. He's not happy, of course. Even though you made him promise I could marry who I liked, he still thought he'd be able to strong-arm me into marrying some baronet or marquess. He hadn't the foggiest idea that I already knew exactly who I wanted to marry. Funny, isn't it?"

"I'm glad Papa and Mama aren't here, really," Prudy confessed. "I don't think Papa and Gideon will get on well. Besides, I'm not silly little Prudy anymore, who always says the wrong thing and isn't pretty enough to make a good match. I'm Lady Rycroft, and I've earned a great deal of respect in this town."

"Indeed you have," Catherine said, squeezing her sister's arm. "I'm so proud of you, truly, I am. And now that I know you love Gideon, I can be *happy* for you, too. You don't know how many nights I tossed and turned, eaten up with guilt because I knew I ought to have had this fate, not you."

"It worked out perfectly," Prudy reassured her sister. "You couldn't have loved Gideon, and frankly, he wouldn't have loved you. We're a match, though. I love him more than words can say."

Catherine's eyes misted up. "Oh, my darling girl, I'm so glad to hear it. I must confess, when I first came here all those months ago, after that Isaac Bates business, I had no idea what to expect. Gideon is strange, but... well, I like him."

Prudy grinned. "I'm glad to hear it, because I like him too."

"Now, if you'll excuse me, I'm going to talk to that friend of yours, Jane."

"That's perfect timing, because I want to go and talk to my husband."

Smiling, Catherine pressed a kiss to her sister's cheek, and moved out into the crowd. That left Prudy free to make her way through her guests to where Gideon stood, sipping a glass of whiskey.

"Enjoying the party?" Prudy asked, looping her arm through his.

"I never do," he sighed, "But *you* are, and I'm glad to see that."

"Excellent. Well, perhaps now would be as good a time as any to deliver some news, my dear husband."

He narrowed his eyes. "Good news or bad news?"

"I suppose we'll find out."

Prudy stood on her tiptoes and kissed Gideon full on the lips, regardless of how shocking it might be.

"My dear Lord Rycroft, we are going to be parents."

Gideon's face blanched. "You mean..."

"Yes. I'm pregnant. Early days, of course, but still."

A smile broke out over his face.

"You're right. That is excellent news. I may, however, need to sit down for a while."

The End

Made in the USA
Monee, IL
05 July 2025

20529388R00101